# Stuck Wit'chu

OLIVIA SHAW-REEL

# 'TIS THE

# SEASON, Y'ALL...

Wintertime is here again, and it is my *absolute* favorite time of the year! This book is not necessarily a HOLIDAY story, but may all who read feel the joy, spirit, and charm of the season. Also, let's remember and celebrate the REAL reason behind the season.

|| Happy Birthday, Jesus! ||

To my family and supporters who continuously love on me and my books – you have been the GREATEST gifts to me, year after year!

From the bottom of my heart: thank you!

*-OSR*

# PROLOGUE: KEITH

My biceps, triceps, and every other muscle in my arms were screaming, but I couldn't play myself in a room full of weightlifters. I had to keep pushing, breathing, and imagining my "summer body" in full effect.

"Sixty...sixty-one. Ah. Sixty-two."

The sounds of the gym were hypnotizing as I worked on my third set of mountain climbers. I had already completed my daily sets of jumping jacks, sit-ups, push-ups, and burpees, and I could stand to challenge myself to more cardio and conditioning.

Music that I wouldn't normally listen to blared from the speakers, and my own music from my own headphones was just as loud in one of my ears. The *tings* of metal slapping against metal was familiar, while gruff sighs and grunts of exhausted men and women rang out almost melodically. The occasional whistle of surrounding treadmills could also be deciphered through the pounding in my head.

"Sixty-six...sixty-seven..."

I lived for these moments. I lived for this alone time of pushing my body to the limits and sweating from just about every pore in my body. As it had always been for me, working out made every wrong thing going on in my life right. It made my mood better, and my day brighter. I wouldn't trade this addiction for anything else in the world.

"Seventy."

I was focused—motivated—and unstoppable. That is, until I heard the most beautiful laugh ring out. My eyes left the sweaty, hunched image of myself and swept the room. My gaze soon landed on an unfamiliar face—one I hadn't seen in all the times I frequented this gym.

I knew from the moment she entered the room that I had to have her. Her compact body, no taller than five feet, it seemed, donned short spandex shorts, a tank top and...ballerina shoes. On her head was a silk scarf tied in a cute little bow, and peeking from it were tendrils of curly dark brown hair. My fingers itched to touch her hair, her skin, and her body. Shoot, anything she had to offer a brotha. To my surprise, she wore a face full of makeup and the women she entered with wore similar getups.

I had to chuckle at how they looked; none of the women were *truly* prepared for a workout. They looked too overdressed and too made up with their jewelry, bright lipstick, and dance shoes. As they checked in at the front desk and then grabbed bottles of water on their way to the locker rooms, I kept my eye on the shortest one. She was intriguing and mysterious, and I didn't know her name. I hoped to change that sooner than later.

Their swinging hips and backsides disappeared behind a row of elliptical machines and for a moment, I was disappointed in the obstructed view. I wanted to see more of them—*well*, more of her. Though beautiful and well put together, Amazon-like women weren't my preference and the pretty lady's friends seemed just shy of six feet. No thanks.

Eventually, I lost sight of the trio completely and dedicated another 15 minutes to my workout before wrapping up. It was time to head out and head home for a nice hot shower and a frozen meat and vegetable dinner. I wasn't one to stick around and shower at the gym or even change for that matter, so I disinfected and wiped down my station, collected my belongings and then waved a goodbye to the college-aged desk attendant. She was a cute blonde, with braces and acne, and had an obvious crush on me. I knew her older siblings well from coming in the gym over the years.

As I walked the short distance to the door, with my head down and my eyes on a couple missed calls, I tripped on something. Someone. A combination of the two, rather.

I nearly fell but caught myself on the edge of the desk. My phone and towel dropped, and the person beneath me moaned in agony as my phone toppled on her unsuspecting head.

It was one of the super tall women who had been with "my girl." She looked fragile as she knelt down, likely tying her pink and black shoe, and I was too much of a gentleman not to help her up and dust her off a bit. We stood at eye level, examining the other for a moment, until our mouths both crinkled with a smile.

"Are you okay?" I was the first to ask, straightening the strap of her shirt.

"I'm fine, just a little stunned. I guess choosing to tie my shoe in an exit way wasn't the brightest decision." She smiled and her teeth were brighter than any set of teeth I've ever seen. Straighter, too. She had the ideal mouth for any orthodontist.

"You're alright. It's my fault for not looking. I didn't loosen up anything in there, did I?" I joked, in reference to her head that she continually rubbed in embarrassment.

"No, no. You're good. She already had a couple loose screws up there," another voice entered our conversation. It was much softer and silkier than the Amazonian in front of me.

I glanced over a shoulder and to my surprise, it was the mysterious woman I'd stared down just minutes before. She was even sexier up close, and she smelled like trouble. Light sweat covered the visible parts of her cappuccino skin. She no longer wore her ballet slippers, and she had stripped down from her tank top to a sports bra that left little to the imagination.

I had to quickly divert my attention, my focus. I began to recite the ABCs and avoided her sultry stare. I took a few steps back to compose myself and cleared my throat, doing everything I could not to make a fool out of myself.

She smiled, her eyes sparkling with amusement. "Are you a resident here?"

"Yeah, I—I'm a regular here. This gym is like a second home to me."

Her friend giggled. She hid her smile behind a hand. "No, no. Are you a resident in the city? Do you live here in the city?"

*Idiot.* I mentally kicked myself.

"Oh! Right. Yes, I live in Durham." My eyebrows bushed together in thought. I was no longer interested in that shower or dinner. Getting to know this woman better was my main goal this evening. "I take it you two don't?"

The Amazonian spoke this time, stretching her tired limbs. I caught a whiff of spearmint on her tongue as she spoke, "We went to college in NYC, where we live now, but our families are from around here."

"Yep, and we're visiting, while on tour, and decided to kick the night off with a workout before hitting the clubs. The night is still young, you know."

They were an ambitious group, I had to give it to 'em. "*Tour*? What exactly do you do?"

The third friend joined them at that moment, and as if this entire conversation had been rehearsed, the three women struck three different poses that resulted in them smiling, arms locked and extended, and their toes pointed at unorthodox angles. Who were they trying to be—the new-age Charlie's Angels?

"We're ballet dancers," they spoke together.

"*Award-winning* ballet dancers," my girl clarified.

*Ahhh.* That explained the odd shoe choices. I nodded, impressed, and frankly, wanting to know more about their tour, their dance history, and whatever else they had to tell me. I was intrigued, and my interest was piqued.

They posed a moment more before falling into one another playfully and breaking out into a fit of giggles. As they leaned into one another, my eyes sought out the shortest one. There was just something about her, something so exciting and refreshing.

"Mmm. That's admirable. I don't think I've ever personally met black ballet dancers, if I can be honest. That's dope."

*And the only famous one I could think of off the top of my head was the late Raven Wilkinson,* I thought. I needed to brush up on my black history.

"We're some of the best you'll ever meet," my girl promised, making my heart jump for another time.

What was it about her that made me blush? I felt like a schoolboy with the effect she had on me. She was so small and petite, but had the power to bring me to my knees, if not for my pride...and my strong calf muscles. Leg day had been good to me the past several years.

I was a gentleman, so I wasn't going to exclude her friends from my forthcoming invite. But I prayed to God that they would take the hint and leave us alone when I proposed it.

"Hey...uh, instead of hitting the clubs, would you ladies like to meet back up and I can treat you to a nice, healthy post workout dinner?" Though I said 'ladies,' my gaze was clearly set on the mystery woman.

All three sets of eyes jerked to meet mine. Smiles faded, and bodies shifted semi-uncomfortably. The woman I'd knocked over decided to be the spokesperson for the group.

"Oh, no, we can't tie up your evening. Thanks for the offer, but we'll stick to our original plans since we're meeting up with some of the other dancers and crew members."

"Aw, that's too bad. I know a great hibachi steakhouse right up the street from my condo." I tucked my phone in my back pocket, and retrieved a business card from my duffel bag. I handed it to the one in the middle. She bit her lip and accepted it. "If you change your mind, that's my phone number. I'm Keith. Give me a call...uh…"

"Monica."

"Tatyana."

"*Marlow.*"

Her name was Marlow. My girl had a gorgeous name; it was just as mysterious as she was.

I smiled and tipped the brim of my cap, something my grandfather taught me when I was younger. I was sure I looked like I had stepped right out of the 1940s with that gesture, but chivalry wasn't dead for the male species. If Justin Timberlake could bring sexy back, I was determined to bring chivalry to the forefront. "Take care, ladies."

I didn't dare look back and give them a winning smile, but in the reflection of the gym windows, I could see Monica and Tatyana turn around and head back in the opposite direction. Marlow stood in the same spot and watched me leave and then tucked my business card in the strap of her sports bra.

I hoped she didn't lose my information.

I was two minutes away from retrieving my TV dinner from the microwave and settling down on my L-shaped couch. The aromas of the pepper steak and rice caused my stomach to rumble with anticipation. Besides the stale, sesame seed bagel I'd half eaten and spit out this morning, I hadn't put much of anything else in my stomach and now my head and body was protesting. I'm sure the hot, steamy shower didn't contribute to the shakiness I now felt from a lack of nourishment either.

The microwave soon beeped, signifying its contents was fully warmed and ready for consumption. Clad in only a thick towel and flip flops, I tucked a two-liter soda under my arm, gathered my meal with a potholder, and then managed to snatch off a napkin with my teeth. I made a beeline through my 1,200-square foot condo and plopped down on the couch.

*Ahhh*. This was the life. Bachelor living at its finest. An empty house was just what I liked on a Friday night. Aw, who was I kidding? I was only making the best out of singleness at 28.

My favorite Will Smith movie was paused on the TV screen and just as my fingers pressed the PLAY button, I heard a knock on the back door. I growled.

Reluctantly leaving my meal and movie, and tightening the towel around my hips, I moseyed to the back door. It couldn't have been anybody I knew because all of my guests knew the back door was off limits. Maybe it was a delivery person who had gotten the addresses mixed up, or a neighbor telling me to look out for the raccoons that we occasionally spotted. Either way, I despised the interruption.

I unlocked and opened my door, expecting some man in a greasy, smelly uniform with a square pizza box in hand. Instead, I was greeted with a feminine silhouette who smelled amazing, as she held up a plastic bag of food in one hand and a wine bottle in her opposite hand.

"I come bearing giiiifts," Marlow greeted me, her voice deeper and raspier than I remembered from the gym. I bet she had an amazing singing voice.

"How did you find me?" Not that I was complaining, but I had to know.

I didn't miss the way her eyes slightly widened and examined me from head to toe, and then again chest to toe, and then finally just leveled on my chest. I chuckled and the motion of my chest heaving up and down broke her attention from my mannish parts.

"Your address was on your card."

"It *was?*" With a frown, I thought back to the glossy card I'd handed her. "It couldn't have been. There's my business address, my phone number, and email...but not my home address."

She shoved the bag of food in my hands, pushed me slightly out of the way, and then presented the business card that she had tucked in her hand. Sure enough, my address was scrawled horizontally there in blue ink. There was also dollar signs and numbers underneath my street number. It all made sense.

"Ooh. I gave you the wrong card. That was for one of the contractors working on my patio. It looks like my business card, but it's not."

"Well, it's a good thing you did, huh? Otherwise I would have been pissed, sitting at your place of business, with all this food and wine and no one to share it with."

I couldn't help but smile, watching her make herself comfortable as though she'd been by the house before. Suddenly, the pepper steak dinner didn't seem so appealing as she pulled out takeout boxes from the hibachi place I intended to take them to.

"I hope you haven't eaten." She tossed her head back and took a whiff into the air. "What am I smelling?"

"Dinner that's about to be thrown out," I joked. "Show me what you've got."

She emptied the bag and I loaded our plates up with spicy tuna rolls, crab rolls, fried tofu, and salmon sushi. I couldn't have asked for a better alternative.

"You're a lifesaver, girl, you know that?"

"I've been told that a time or two." She winked.

"Where did your girls end up going?"

"Monica said she was tired, and Tatyana headed to the club still, but I wasn't feeling that tonight. I was ready to put on a movie and order some room service, but then I saw your business card and decided to be spontaneous."

"I'm glad you did."

"I'm glad I did too." She tore off a few napkins from the dispenser.

"How long will you be in my neck of the woods?"

"Just until Monday. We have a show in Charlotte that evening. Thankfully, we get two days off and then we will be heading to Tampa on Thursday. I love touring," she admitted, sneaking a quick bite of an egg roll, "but it can get pretty exhausting."

"I can only imagine. It seems fun. You get to travel the world, meet new people, try new experiences, and yet...it's..."

"*Exhausting*," she finished off again, laughing. "My sleep schedule will never be the same after this, but I can't complain. I'm living my dream and many would probably kill to be in my shoes. I don't take this assignment likely."

"Amen, sista." I watched her eat and appreciated the fact that she didn't care how she looked. She was already comfortable stuffing her mouth in front of me.

"How long have you been dancing, if you don't mind me asking?"

"Of course not." She paused as she dipped her crab roll in a special red sauce that I was unfamiliar with. "Oh goodness. Let's see...I'm 27, so it'll be 24 years in December. My first dance lesson took place when I was a toddler. It was for our preschool Christmas play that my mom forced me to be in. I ended up falling in love with it and pursuing it seriously."

"Dooope." I nodded appreciatively, taking in the tiny dimple in her right cheek that threatened to further steal my heart. "Someday you've got to show me some footage of you dancing."

"Someday, huh? So there's an intent to see me after this?" She raised her eyebrows in question.

"I *meeean*, anything's possible if you play your cards right," I teased.

She leaned in so close that our noses nearly touched. Her eyes sparkled, flitting back and forth, forth and back, between my line of vision and my lips. I swallowed my bite of food in anticipation for what was next. She couldn't be this bold, could she?

"Unfortunately for you, Keith, I don't play cards."

With that, she leaned back, winked again, and then strolled confidently with her food and drink into the living room. She looked to be in her comfort zone, tucking her shapely legs beneath her, spreading out her food, and picking up where she left off.

By then, the TV had gone to sleep and a screensaver danced around. I could only shake my head in disbelief. She was something else.

"Now! What are we watching?"

"I hope you like Hitch." I followed her lead, plopping down beside her, and my eyes studied her expression. I'd only watched this movie about 70 or 80 times but she didn't have to know.

"Ah! That's my favorite Will Smith movie!" Her eyes lit up as she whipped her head around. "And don't let me get started on how GORGEOUS Eva Mendes is."

She went into how much of a superfan she was of Willard Carroll Smith Jr., and how the lessons taught on *The Fresh Prince of Bel-Air* helped shape her childhood, adolescence, and even adulthood.

As a fellow superfan of the comedian-rapper-actor, I couldn't help but to gawk and smile and nod in agreement.

It was at that moment I fell in love with the most beautifully put together woman I had ever met.

I still remember our vows,
and the sacred oaths we took.
I still remember how our love story commenced,
like a best-selling romance book.
Wrapped up in your arms,
is still the safest place I can be.
Wrapped up in your warmth and love;
is where I'll stay for eternity.

Can we please go back to that day in December?
The excitement,
the innocence,
the willingness,
the vigor…

Nothing changed but our ages,
and we're gracefully aging together.
Nothing could tear me from you;
we're two lovers flocked forever.
Baby, even now, years later...
Your touch is so tender.
Baby, even now, years later...
I still remember.

# CHAPTER 1: MARLOW

*Twelve years later...*

I watched Keith slurp my leftover pasta down as if it was the last meal he would ever eat on earth. As if he hadn't just devoured a steak with caramelized onions, sautéed mushrooms, and spinach. As if he was a *freakin'* five-year-old untrained child.

Tonight, we had gone to our favorite Italian restaurant and gotten full midway through our entrees. He had since taken my dinner from the Styrofoam to-go container, and dumped it into his favorite bowl—the gigantic bowl that was previously designated for fresh chopped vegetables or salads, but that he'd made into a cereal bowl.

I watched him balance it on his barely there stomach, his large hands gripping the bowl not as securely as I wanted. I couldn't help but to tighten my jaw, clamp down on my teeth, and ball my fists until my knuckles whitened. This was an accident waiting to happen and who would be the one to clean it up after it spilled? Yep. Me.

Honestly, he wasn't half bad looking in his fitting red T-shirt, loose fitting jeans, red and white kicks, and the red cap that was turned backwards on his head. Red had always been his color. It brought out his brilliant undertones and made his brown eyes pop. Plus, the tiny curls peeking from his cap made my fingers itch to twirl the short and thick tresses. He was growing his hair out for whatever reason and it looked good on him. Darn good.

But as I continued to eye him with irritation, I knew my contempt ran much deeper than looks and slurping. I was unhappy—we both were. After 10 years of marriage, three children, and two careers that were pulling us in opposite directions, I knew it was time to call it quits. Keith wasn't as vocal or obvious as I was regarding my disinterest and desire to move on, but I knew he felt the same.

It was in our touches; it was in our kisses. It was in our rushed love making that lacked passion and tenderness. It was in our tense conversations and awkward family dinners. It was now getting the best of us. He was tired and I was beyond exhausted with trying to fight for what remained.

At some point, whether married or in a general relationship, either the man or woman had to take the lead and save the other from destruction. My proposal to split wasn't received well initially, but nowadays we couldn't wait to go forward with those plans with our family attorney.

Our eldest children, Harlee and David—named after Keith's obsession with Harley Davidson motorcycles— had been walking around lately with long faces. It's like they, too, realized the thrill was gone. Their parents were splitting and separate households would soon become their reality. At nine and eight, it had to be confusing, frustrating, and disappointing to witness the countless arguments and disagreements between us that we tried so desperately to avoid.

On the other hand, our five-year-old, Shalom, was clueless and still looked at her mommy and daddy as heroes. In her bright honey-brownish eyes, we truly could do no wrong. I wanted that innocence to stay forever but it was only a matter of time before she also saw our marriage and feigned cordiality for the foolishness that it was.

The kids all sat at the other end of the table; it was Friday, which meant it was family night. It was the *one* night we got to spend together, free of homework and projects, dance rehearsals and sports, clients and conference calls, and whatever else life threw our way during the chaotic week.

Whether I cooked, or we picked up something to eat, we would all sit at the table, talk about our days, and then retire into our home theater for ice cream and a movie. It was a tradition Keith and I set from the first day we met. Today would be no exception, and I planned to make the most of our time together, since it was only a matter of time before these moments ended.

Keith slurped the remaining traces of marinara sauce from the plastic spoon, soon tossing it and the to-go box away. He stood up from the table, his handprints smudging against the glass, and disappeared into the kitchen briefly. He soon emerged with a canned dark soda, his eyes immediately finding mine where I continued to stare him down.

He nearly choked as he saw my dissatisfied look. He sighed deeply as he placed his can on the table. Dark brown liquid slightly flew from the can opening with the force. "What did I do *now*?"

"Don't do that," I hissed. "I haven't said a word."

"You didn't have to. Your face and attitude says it all. Can't we just have one night of peace? Dang, 'Low. Just...let it go. Whatever's got your panties in a bunch, please. Just let it go. I'm tired. I had a long week. I don't need," he motioned with his large hands, "this."

My eyebrows shot up in surprise, and the amateur boxer in me seemed to want to make her presence known. No, I wasn't going to physically hit him, but more often than not, I was always ready for an argument or two...or ten.

"You don't need *what*? I haven't even said anything, because if you knew even an INKLING of what was on my mind, you wouldn't be..."

"Mommy? Daddy? Come on. Movie's starting!"

Shalom proved to be our saving grace as she wedged herself between our worn bodies. My words dissipated.

She grabbed each of our hands and tugged us in the direction of the theater. The twins, as we called them—since they favored one another almost identically—were setting up shop. The popcorn machine was warming up, previews to an action movie were playing, and the lights had dimmed significantly.

All of these features made our home theater one of the best in the city and dare I say, THEE best on the block.

"Can I sit on your lap?" Shalom begged with purposefully large eyes and a pouty mouth. She knew exactly what she was doing with all of her natural, innocent beauty. The same look had gotten her out of trouble before on way too *many* occasions that I cared to admit.

I nodded, already prepared to give her my usual "yes, Princess," but she hit me with something new for the first time. She looked at her father and then grinned up at him.

"And can you sit by us too, Daddy?"

Keith normally sprawled out on the floor and obnoxiously stretched his long limbs out. He returned her smile and reluctantly nodded after consulting silently with me. I figured the close proximity could not hurt us.

"Uh, sure, baby girl. We can all sit together." He leaned down to scoop her up in his arms. She squealed and tossed her head back as he proceeded to tickle her.

As beautiful as they looked together, I pulled away to tend to the buzz of my cell phone. I retrieved the device from the pocket of my stretch pants and swiped to answer.

"Hello?"

"Giiiiirl, I have the GREATEST news!" Monica's voice was shrill and unexpected.

I braced myself, knowing she wouldn't be this excited over something miniscule. We had not talked since the closing night of our last tour, which ended more than two months ago. Though still the greatest of friends since middle school, she, too, kept busy with her own life, family, and obligations. However, we knew that we loved each other and were one call away, if need be.

"Tatyana's here with me too. I have you on speakerphone."

I smiled warmly with my thoughts on the women. Like Monica, Tatyana and I also met in middle school. We all were new to the performing arts school and just as shy as can be, but our love for dance drew us together. When given the opportunity to work together in a mid-semester recital, we bonded and had been inseparable since. After going to college on the East Coast, we'd all graduated and relocated back to the good old South. Now, we were all married with children and living out our dance dreams. Life was a trip.

Monica and her brain surgeon husband were celebrating six years and had a toddler and first grader; Tatyana was content with her construction-working high school sweetheart and their son. They were celebrating nine years this fall. Of my girls, my marriage was the longest but rockiest. The women knew of some of our troubles, but for the most part, I had yet to explain how far apart Keith and I had grown over the last year. This, of course, was a conversation for another time and place.

"Okay, you're calling me during family night, so it *must* be important." I looked over a shoulder, gauging the TV screen. "I have like...four minutes until one of these Marvel movies start playing, so talk quickly."

I settled in my usual front row and center spot, and Shalom wasted no time climbing in my lap and planting her curly head of hair in the crook of my neck. From the corner of my eye, I saw Keith settle two seats away. He sighed heavily, and then crossed his arms over his chest comfortably. The twins were scattered somewhere behind us, as they animatedly discussed how fearless Captain *Somebody* was. I couldn't remember these character names to save my life.

"Oh! Right! Family night, I forgot. Sorry," Monica apologized, her voice lowering only decimals. There was still a dash of excitement in her tone. "We won't be long."

Tatyana butted in for the first time. "How does late September and early October look for you? I know you're big on getting a heads up, but 22 days is the most I can do. This was just kind of presented to us and we wanted to share it with you."

"Uhh..." My forehead wrinkled in thought. "I don't have anything planned, per se. Shalom starts virtual kindergarten the week of Labor Day; the twins start back that same week. Ummm, other than that, I can't think of anything else at the moment."

Keith tensed up and shifted beside me, likely eavesdropping.

"Girl! That's perfect then. You won't believe what we have lined up."

"I'm...waiting on the news," I teased. "Is it a show? What? What? Somebody talk!"

My interest was piqued, no doubt, but my brooding husband took some of that excitement away as I gave him a questioning stare. He shook his head and I could literally feel the heat from his body. Whatever.

"Even better!" Monica squeaked before she yelled, "We're going to be on TV, baby!"

I sat up a little straighter in the leather loveseat, holding onto my heart with one hand, balance the phone between my cheek and shoulder, and placing my hand around Shalom so that she wouldn't tumble from my lap. It was a task that only a mother could handle.

"TV? What do you mean? We've been on TV before."

"No, no. Primetime, bay-bee! Prime...time! The tour was selected for a two-hour live special on a major network. Which one, we don't know yet, but we fly out to Tampa to start choreography at the end of September and sometime in early October, we start filming. The actual show will air around Christmastime."

If it were possible for my heart to leave my body, it would have. My hand trembled as I pressed my ear closer to the phone. Somewhere behind me, the twins were getting a little rowdier; Shalom started asking for her ice cream, and Keith continued scoffing. He had likely heard every word because Monica could be a loud mouth at times. Okay, *most* times, she was a loud mouth.

Yet and still, I could not understand his attitude—he knew my career called for unexpected trips and time away from home. This time was no different.

"Oh...my goodness. This is huge! And you know all of this *how*?"

Tatyana giggled. "You sound like me. I always forget the choreographer and director of the show are Monica's cousins. They gave her the scoop just as we were about to head out for drinks, and you know she can't hold water."

"Drinks? Oh, Lord. Don't you two overdo it."

I could practically hear the eye roll through the phone. "Yes, Mother. I'm sure at 39 and three-quarters I know my limits."

"Yeah, but Monica doesn't."

"Uhm, I'm sitting RIGHT here," Monica whined.

"I'm just teasin', but seriously. Be careful with this virus going on. Cases aren't going down."

"Honey, chile, we *knooow*," Tatyana growled playfully.

"Anyway, y'all know I had to say something ahead of time. It wouldn't be right. We do have an all-staff, all-crew members' video call next week, so just act surprised when Grant gives us the rundown."

"Will do," I chuckled.

"Mommyyyy," Shalom whined, her lips close to my available ear. "We have to get our ice cream! Remember?"

"Tell my baby love 'hello'. We'll let you go," Tatyana purred, "And tell that fine hunk of a man 'hello,' as well, from his favorite person in the whole wide world."

I glanced over in Keith's direction. "Taty says hello and called you fine."

"Coming from her, that makes me nauseous," he mumbled, though there was a playful spark in his eye. They had always gone back and forth playfully over the years. Their relationship reminded me a lot of Martin and Pam from *The Martin Lawrence Show*. Though they ribbed each other to no end, they still deeply loved and respected one another through it all.

I giggled and ended the call shortly after. The movie was just beginning and Shalom was nearly in tears because her cookies and cream ice cream was nowhere in sight. The twins were now shoveling buttery, piping hot popcorn into their designated bowls and racing each other to the mini refrigerator for drinks.

I decided to be generous and offered, "Keith, you need anything while I'm up?"

"Just an explanation on what that call was about," he said simply, his eyes never leaving the 70-inch TV.

I gave him a small, sarcastic smile. "As if you didn't hear anything, right? You were clearly eavesdropping, so you know exactly what Monica and Taty had to say." I rolled my eyes and carried on. "This is my final offer: do you need anything while I'm up?"

Keith growled lowly and stood up. The motion was so sudden that I cried out in surprise, as he cuffed me by the elbow and ushered me into the kitchen. When we were out of earshot, I snatched my arm from him and gave him a crazy look.

"Have you lost your mind?" I questioned, though I really wanted to tell him if he grabbed me so roughly again, I'd smack him upside the head. We weren't physical or violent towards each other in the least, and never had been, but I understood how anger made us do idiotic things.

"I can ask you that same thing. What are we doing these days? Why are you so snappy and disrespectful, and showing out in front of the kids lately?"

"And dragging me out of the room by my arm isn't? I hate how you always turn things around and make it seem like I'm the only one doing wrong. We've both been at each other's throats lately, and we both are on edge. Stop acting like you don't know why."

"That's just it. WHY are we walking around on eggshells, Marlow? Why can't we talk through our problems like before? When did things change for us, baby? That's all I want to know. Where...did we go wrong?"

I looked him in the eye as his voice broke, feeling slightly lightheaded and overwhelmed. He shook his head in disbelief and looked away, focusing somewhere on the upper cabinets and the ceiling fan.

"So what's up with this new gig? It's amazing that, not once in the conversation, did you consult with me. It's disappointing that you just agreed to something without talking to me first, and it's selfish that..."

"What, Keith? That I pushed aside my motherly and wifely duties to pursue more of my dreams? That I thought of only me first? Which one is it this time?" I antagonized, studying his rigid face and unhappy expression. "What did I do now?"

Keith's eyes stayed on me until I was forced to blink to moisten them. To my surprise, the corners of his perfect lips slid up into a half smile. He shook his head in incredulity, chuckled bitterly, and then turned on his socked feet.

"If you can't figure out WHY I'm upset, then you really are the problem," he threw over a shoulder. He ambled back into the theater without another word, coolly scooping up Shalom and blowing raspberries on her stomach.

"He says I'm the one who's tripping, but he's just as bad. I don't get it," I said to myself.

"Please don't go to bed angry. Just let him cool down and you guys can revisit the conversation another time," I heard softly, looking down at my phone in confusion.

"What in the world…*hello*?"

I noticed the call from my friends was still very much going on, nearing 12 minutes. I hadn't hung up as I thought and neither had my good friends. Both Monica and Tatyana had heard our disagreement and harsh exchanges, and I was so embarrassed that I could only swipe and end the call—for good, this time—and collapsed on the floor in a heap of tears.

As I wept and sniffled, and wiped and repeated, my mind went back to a more innocent time. I travelled back to a moment in history where arguments were far and few; I thought back to a time before wedding bells, and the years of courting and getting to know one another. I reminisced on the time before we had our children. The kids were our blessings and greatest joys, but things weren't so complicated then. Things weren't so tense and confusing and frustrating. Things made sense.

I missed us. But I knew "us" seemed to be no more and that thought hurt more than anything.

As with most Marvel movies, two and a half hours passed before the ending credits rolled. Shalom snored softly with her head on my lap and her legs thrown over her father's. The twins were also asleep, their bodies leaned into one another and their bowls of popcorn carelessly tossed to the floor. Keith stopped the movie and turned off the TV so that we were in complete darkness and silence. His breathing was even and calm, and his eyes remained forward, but his attention was on me.

"Ready to head up?" His husky question broke through the stillness.

I nodded as though he could see me, and gathered Shalom's 52 pounds of love in my arms, while he woke up the twins and led them to their adjoining bedrooms.

After tucking, kissing, and praying over our babies, I was the first to walk away and enter our master bedroom. Earth tones and soft light greeted me as I undressed, not bothering to hide from Keith, as he finally retired to the room as well.

I was his wife, after all, and we had seen each other in all facets, under all circumstances, and in every angle. There was nothing new to be discovered. I had the same full breasts with a slight drop from breastfeeding three babies, a jiggle to my belly, stretch marks in random places, and smooth brown skin that flushed as he watched me across the room.

"Look, I don't know what's going on, or what's about to happen to...us. But for tonight, can we please...*please* just have a peaceful night? We will discuss everything again tomorrow, okay? I know I upset you, and..."

Keith shushed me and I immediately obliged. With his index finger over his lips, he walked over to me until my naked body was flush against his. Large, warm hands splayed across the dip of my back, before one worked its way up my spine until he could rub the nape of my neck. He cradled me tenderly, for the first time in a long time.

Naturally, by the heaviness of his eyelids, the quicken of his breath, and the look in his eyes, I assumed he was ready to kiss me. But then he lowered his head against the side of mine. He turned his face and trailed kisses along my reddening skin, and whispered, "You still don't know, do you?"

"Uh...Know *what?*" At that point, I was still upset but now very turned on and confused. In my mind, Keith should have been undressing, instead of questioning me.

All at once, our embrace dissipated and the moment was lost—gone forever. Keith slipped his arms away and my nipples brushed rashly against his shirt, invoking a yelp of pain. He eyed me with the same incredulity as before and shook his head.

"God, Marlow! For once...just ONCE, think about someone other than yourself!"

"I *was* thinking about you! I was thinking about making love to you, for goodness sake! What's gotten into you?"

"What's gotten into me? What's gotten into ME?" Keith chuckled lowly. "Wow."

"Why can't you tell me what I did? Or what I'm doing? Is it so wrong for me—a mother of three, who has sacrificed so much for this family, to continue to pursue her goals? You have your projects and businesses and they're flourishing, so why can't I do something for me?"

His eyes narrowed to slits as I spoke.

"This opportunity doesn't come around often for people like me, and you KNOW this has been my dream for a while. I don't understand why you're so upset."

Keith nodded and headed for the door. He pointed and gritted through perfect white teeth, "And THAT is my problem." The door slammed behind him.

I could either follow behind him where we whisper-yelled, so we didn't wake the kids, or I could go into the bathroom and shower off the day's frustrations. I chose the latter, which had been my original plan, and I stayed inside of the shower for as long as I wanted, knowing Keith probably wouldn't be up for a while. I anticipated that he may even fall asleep in the den, as he had done so many other times when we shared a disagreement.

As I dried off, moisturized and performed my other nightly duties, my eyes skimmed the length of the bathroom. It was immaculate and everything I could have ever wanted, from the natural stone walls, to the freestanding oval tub, to the glass wall dividers and the spacious shower; everything was perfect. From blueprint to construction, this home had become the manifestation of our hard work, love, and labor.

I continued to admire myself as I pulled a pair of panties out of my bathroom closet, along with a modest nightgown. I pulled my garments on, searching briefly for my satin headscarf. It was over by the cute little calendar that Shalom had handcrafted for us in daycare. We had the 12-month booklet propped up by the mirror and she had circled all the important dates with crayon, with obvious help from her teachers and siblings. I walked over and reached for the scarf, my eyes doubling back over to the calendar as something bright yellow caught my eye.

I dropped the scarf, and my heart fell right along with it, as I realized not only why my husband was upset, but just how much of an idiot I was.

# CHAPTER 2: MARLOW

The stench of burning bacon grease woke me up the next morning, and naturally, I shot up in bed with alarm. I was normally the Saturday morning cook, so I was surprised to hear and smell that food was being cooked without me.

"Keith?"

My husband didn't answer, so I rushed to find a robe and slippers, and headed downstairs.

"Harlee? David?"

I doubted the kids were even up, but it was good to call out their names, just in case. I zipped past their rooms, seeing half ajar doors, mangled sheets, and legs and arms hanging off of their beds.

"*Shalom?* Lord knows YOU better not be in that kitchen."

My future kindergartner was asleep, tucked soundly amongst her favorite stuffed animals, in the place I had left her. Good.

As I rounded the corner, Keith stood in front of the gas stovetop, with just sweatpants on and a bare chest. Bacon had overcooked in one of the skillets, proving my sense of smell was spot on.

"Morning. You need some help in here?"

Keith paused as he lightly scraped the cheesy egg, green pepper and onion mix from another skillet onto a plate, with only his eyes blinking, and his chest moving up and down.

"I'm done, but thank you."

"You sure?" I asked shyly, under his scrutiny. Maybe if I made a joke, I wouldn't seem like such an idiot for my mistakes. If I made him crack a smile, I wouldn't seem like such a bad wife for completely forgetting the plans we had made this time last year. If I made him laugh, I definitely wouldn't seem like such a selfish person for once again putting my dreams "before our family" as he so eloquently put it.

"It looks like your bacon is burning," I added.

His head jerked to the left side of the stove, and his eyes widened at my discovery. Sure enough, the pork was sizzling and popping, and a thin layer of char was developing.

He mumbled something under his breath, rushing to put down the egg skillet and then turning off the eye where the bacon was. "Thanks," he told me, chuckling.

I continued to watch him move around the kitchen with ease—buttering the biscuits, tucking aluminum foil around the sausage links, pulling mason jars of jellies out of the fridge, and pouring half cups of orange juice around the table.

One thing I loved about Keith was he could throw down in the kitchen. I didn't feel as overwhelmed as a wife with him in my life because he was a natural provider and homemaker. I knew if we weren't together, he was still going to be alright financially, emotionally, and just overall. He took care of home, and his kids meant the world to him. I couldn't have asked for a better life partner and children's father.

It was now or never. I had to address the elephant in the room. I smoothed my hands along the countertop and then leaned forward.

"Listen, I wanted to apologize for yesterday, baby. I jumped the gun; I didn't consider your feelings, and I...I messed up, okay? I promise I'll call the director and tell him the show will have to go on without me." I cleared my throat. "I know that it's around the time of your birthday trip, and we have plans already, and I'm…looking forward to going with you and the kids."

Keith wiped his well-sculpted and purely masculine hands on the towel draped around the refrigerator handle. His back was to me as he pulled down the bottle of syrup from a top cabinet.

"You'd really do that for me?"

"I would do it for US." I nodded, though he couldn't see me. "No question."

"Do it then," he said simply, turning to face me again. He leaned against the counter, motioning towards his phone that lay feet away. "Call him now. In front of me."

"*Now*? We're ready to eat."

"The kids aren't down yet, and I haven't put anything on plates. You're good." He slid the phone towards me. "I'll step out if you..."

"You don't have to." We didn't keep very many secrets from one another, if at all. We certainly didn't tiptoe around the house or sneak on phone calls, so him standing in while I called my boss was not a big deal. It was the "I told you so" energy that I knew my friends would later give me that I wasn't looking forward to.

"*He controls too much of your career,*" and "*Girl, my husband would never deny me this opportunity,*" were some of the things my friends told me all the time.

Keith stepped out to call the kids down, as I dialed the familiar seven digits. It rang once, twice, and then went to voicemail. I wouldn't dare leave a message of such importance on his answering service, but I did tell the director to return the call on my phone and that it was urgent.

"What'd he say?" Keith wanted to know, leaning against the doorframe.

"He didn't answer. I'll let you know once he calls back."

"Cool." Keith clapped his hands once, and looked at the table where the kids were getting situated, half asleep, and half coherent.

Shalom's hair was a mess and had tangled throughout the night; Harlee's pajamas were twisted as she yawned loudly into a hand, and David was wiping the crust from his eyes as he blindly walked and plopped down in his usual middle seat.

I giggled, my heart swelling with joy. My babies looked rough, but they were just that. *My* babies. I knew, in that moment, that there was no place I would rather be, and not even my passion for dance could make me leave their sides.

It was a couple hours later when the director returned my call, and in fact, it was his assistant who was on the other line as I delivered the bad news that I would not be joining the show. Though disappointed, she was also understanding, and told me she would miss my energy and presence on the stage. After so many years of working closely together, it was evident that we were all like family. One missing piece in the 200-member crew was always felt.

Once that was out of the way, I sent a message to me and the girls' group chat retracting my statement that I'd be joining the show. Then, knowing they would each call and scold me in some form or fashion, I turned off the phone.

I sighed and collapsed back onto the bed, inches away from a jumble of washcloths and bath towels in dark hues. The laundry could wait. My heart was broken.

"You're doing the right thing," I heard above me.

I didn't look at my husband but knew he was only trying to convince me not to overthink and regret my decision.

"Yeah," I whispered, "But why do I feel so bad?"

"Hey, I'll take care of the laundry if you can run to the store for me. Can you make some smothered porkchops tonight?" Keith asked, stepping closer to the bed and catching my eye. He gave me a charming smile. "*Please?*"

I rolled my eyes, though I was unable to stop myself from agreeing. As much as he annoyed me half the time, I couldn't resist that smile or his kind request. My family loved my good ole Southern-styled cooking, and I enjoyed preparing it for them.

"Just text me what you want as a side. I'll see if the kids want to come with me."

David and Harlee were up for the grocery store, while Shalom wanted to stay back and hang with her father. That was fine with me; I had less bodies to look after in the bustling supermarket.

"Masks on," I reminded my children, double-checking my purse for sanitizer and towelettes. "You know the deal."

The coronavirus was still alive and well, and thankfully, our family had not been directly affected by it. Schooling was different, and life looked different, but we had been fortunate not to lose any jobs or other income; our mortgage was still paid each month, and our health was as good as it had been before the pandemic started. I could not complain.

We kept the trip under 20 minutes, stopping only through a few aisles, and then picking up a few pounds of fresh porkchops. I planned on making scalloped potatoes, collard greens, and cornbread for my sides, as requested by Harlee.

"Baby, load up for me, while I find this card," I told David, sifting through my purse, and pushing aside the stray pieces of gum, tissue, old receipts and whatever else I'd thrown into the bag over the last few months.

He did as told, playfully pulling on Harlee's hair. She barely helped him, since her  face was buried in my phone, playing some downloaded game.

Finally, I found my debit card and wallet tucked in a compartment I wouldn't have normally had it, and sighed.

"How are you guys doing today?" the cashier, an elderly woman, asked. Even behind her mask, we could sense her friendly eyes and kind smile.

"Doing okay, yourself?"

"Oh, just fine, baby. Your total, after savings, is $33.56." She bagged up the last few things, and handed them to David. "Such a nice young man, you are. You make sure you be the man of the house and help your mother out, you hear?"

Harlee looked up from the phone she held, lifting a dark eyebrow at the woman's words. David gave her a strange look, cocking his head to the side. Before I could speak up, he was already setting things straight in his pre-adolescence voice, "My *father* is the man of our house," he corrected her.

"Oh! I am so sorry." She looked to me, and then down at the kids sheepishly. "That's what I get for butting in folks' business. My husband tells me all the time to stop doing that."

I swiped my debit card and completed the transaction on the keypad, being sure to pump a few squirts of sanitizer in my palm afterward. "It's alright. You didn't know."

She watched me as I slid my plastic currency back into my wallet, and tucked it into my purse. Her eyes widened slightly. "Wait a minute, did I read that correctly? Marlow Richmond—I only know of one Marlow, and that's my best friend's daughter. Tell me you aren't Jeffie Lee's daughter!"

I had to chuckle at the woman still *butting in folks' business*; though, at least her facts were correct this time. "Yes, that's my mother. I take it you're an old friend of hers?"

"Oh, honey, we go *waaay* back!" If at all possible, her voice became louder and drew the eyes and attention of other customers. It was no wonder her line was the longest; she was talkative with *every* patron. "We mistakenly liked the same boy back in high school, and became good friends in college, years later. I ended up marrying him, but obviously, she has done well for herself too. You are beautiful! Your mother was gorgeous too, but you must look like your father. Jeffie didn't have those cheekbones or that build."

The woman briefly pulled her *Biden/Harris* mask down so that I could see her face completely. She was smiling from ear to ear, and I could spot a couple silver crowns in her mouth from where I stood.

"You tell her Callie Mae said 'hello,' you hear?"

Accepting the receipt she handed me, I gave her a wink and smiled behind my face covering. "Thank you for your hospitality, Mrs. Callie—I'll be sure to tell her you said 'hello.' You take care!"

"Are you and your husband looking to get away at all? My husband, Johnnie, and I, usually go up to our cottage in the Smoky Mountains for the holidays, but this year, with the virus, we're staying put." She propped a hand on her hip, and waved her other hand back and forth while she talked. "It's open and available if you want somewhere to go. Call me sometime, baby. Here, take down my number…it's…"

Tossing an apologetic look at the people behind me, I quickly punched in the woman's number into my phone, and then practically pushed the kids towards the exit. "Got it! Thank you! See you later!"

We were barely out of the doors before we all laughed at Mrs. Callie's antics. She was super sweet but something else.

A smile remained on my face, as we made our way across the crowded parking lot. It only screwed up into a "what the heck?!" expression as I saw a woman literally leaning on the passenger door of the car as if she was paying part of the car note. I gripped my mace a little tighter and stepped in front of my kids.

"Um, excuse me? Please get off of my car."

No sooner than I called that out did the lanky figure turn towards us. The lower part of the woman's face was covered with a face covering and her hair was tucked under a leopard print fedora. She wore a leather coat that barely brushed the small of her back, but I knew exactly who was beneath the dark sunglasses, hat and protective equipment.

"Monica? What are you doing here?"

"I stopped in to pick up a few snacks for the kids, and saw your car. I didn't want to interrupt your shopping trip so I waited out here while Yusuf and the kids went inside." She tucked her phone in her pocket and greeted Harlee and David. "Hey, guys. How y'all doing?"

"Hey, Auntie Monica," they spoke in unison sweetly.

I tucked the few bags we had in the trunk and told them to wait inside for me. It wasn't too chilly out, but I knew Monica had a mouthful considering I had avoided her calls.

She eased her fedora off, revealing a slicked ponytail that hung low down her back. She brushed her fingers along the sides of her head, moving tendrils of hair behind each ear thoughtfully, "I can't say I'm happy about you deciding not to do this show. I also can't say I don't understand your reasoning, because I do. But Marlow, this is everything you've prayed for. This could be our big break. *Your* big break."

"Monica..."

"Hear me out, hear me out. You are the star of the show basically. Your understudy is excellent, don't get me wrong, but nobody can dance like you. *Nobody* can bring to life our show like you can."

"I know, but..."

"That's just it, girl." Monica sighed behind her mask, one she'd sewn and designed herself. "I don't have to say anything more. You know this is a once in a lifetime deal, and all I wanted to do was make that clear. Please don't feel guilty for what you'll miss over the next few months. If 2020 has taught us nothing else, it's taught us the importance of time and doing what we love, with the people who love us. Obviously, your family comes first in all things, but..."

"It's not that, it's just..."

"But," Monica continued, putting her hand up, "You have sacrificed everything for that man. You moved from New York City, the hub of opportunity, back to our country bumpkin upbringing to accommodate your man. Then when he was ready to relocate, you packed up and left again. You even turned down a teaching gig at the biggest performing arts school on the East Coast because he wanted to pursue his athletic dreams, and where did that leave you?"

"Don't...start that," I warned.

"It left you barefoot and pregnant. Three times!" She gave me a knowing look, "And don't you tell me that I did the same thing, because through it all, my husband gave me his blessing to pursue my dreams. I've never had to check in with Yusuf like you do with Keith."

Wind whipped around us, and the warmth of Monica's breath could be seen in the chilly Durham afternoon. It was unusually cool today, matching the iciness of Monica's stare.

"You don't understand. I—"

She interrupted me for a third time, "Your kids and your husband should understand and support that. With the way this virus is going, who knows if we will even tour again, anytime soon? What if we're put on lockdown and this was your only chance to be on prime time? Who knows where this show will lead us? Think it over thoroughly, not for me or Taty, or even your family...but for you. Marlow, will you do that at least?"

I couldn't get a word in edgewise, and Monica was already moving on and asking me what I planned to make for dinner. I ran down my menu, while she nodded and looked off into the distance.

"That sounds so good. You'll have to tell me how it turns out." She stood up a little straighter and put her fedora back on. "I see Yusuf coming now, and he clearly bought way too much. Those kids always talk him into buying extra stuff."

"Uh, Monica? You have a two-year-old and a five-year-old; I'm pretty sure that was all Yusuf's doing," I giggled, looking at his multiple bags of chips and other snacks.

She shook her head in amusement, and though her sunglasses were a chocolate tint, I could see the excitement she still had for her man. It was evident they were still crazy about one another. For a tiny moment—as quickly as a blink of an eye—I felt jealousy before I tucked it away.

"Well, I'll let you go before he comes up and thinks I was trying to pull you over to the dark side."

"But that's exactly what you were doing," I laughed and gave her an elbow pump, something we did to replace our usual hugs and kisses.

"Call me in a few days. Take care, girl."

"You too." I waved to Yusuf and the kids and then climbed in my car to head home. I looked in the rearview at Harlee and David as I spoke, "Guys, your Auntie Monica is something else, you know that?"

"Momma, we know," they said in unison, seconds before we all broke out in laughter.

It wasn't until later that night that I revisited Monica's words. I'd fed and entertained my family, and now the kids were winding down in the den with their electronic devices, books and toys. They had about an hour of free time before I sent them off to get washed up for bed, and then as a family, we would meet back up and pray and read stories together in Shalom's room. As everyone grew older and busier, I knew it was only a matter of time before these special moments came to an end, but for now, I cherished them.

In the meantime, I needed to talk to Keith about what was on my mind. I had to come with my A-game—so after my shower, I sprayed a few mists of perfume, eased my silkiest and shortest nightgown over my body, and pulled my hair up how Keith loved it. We hadn't been intimate in weeks, and when we did, things just weren't the fireworks and magic they once were. I wasn't even sure if my husband even still found me attractive, but I needed a distraction.

I found him leaving out of our home gym, sweaty, and his head downcast. He emerged from the shadows of the lower level, wiping his forehead with the towel draped around his neck, and breathing unevenly. My eyes swept over him, appreciating him and taking him in. I hoped I didn't make a fool of myself as I relaxed against the wall and gave my best "sexy look." You know, the one with the parted, pouty mouth, heavy eyelids, and slightly arched back.

He looked up, paused abruptly, and then gave a light chuckle. "You scared me. What are you doing?"

"Hey, baby."

"Hi." Keith eyed me up and down again and again, lingering on my legs and chest each time. "That new?"

"New because you've never seen it, but I bought it a while ago." I did a cute little twirl. "You like?"

He gave me a strange look, cocking his head to the side. "I was always a fan of you in lingerie, but...*why?*"

*Deflate my ego, why don't you?* I thought, taking a deep breath. *Here goes nothing...*

"I think we should...leave the kids to their devices and...spend a few minutes to ourselves." I grabbed his hands, pulling him towards me. He walked forward until our chests meshed together. "You know, be spontaneous like we used to be."

"I'm a little tired, I'm not gonna lie. I wouldn't have gone so hard in my work out if I knew you were trying to get worked out," he flirted, allowing one hand to roam freely down my back and over the curve of my butt. He pulled me closer. "Mmm...no underwear either?"

"No underwear. Easy access," I giggled, sliding my hands up the front of his chest. They didn't stop moving until they reached his neck. Only then did I circle around to the back of his neck and played with the smooth, tiny hairs there.

"You aren't usually this feisty."

"You don't always look this good to me."

Keith chuckled, resting each hand on the fullness of my bottom. "Mmm, is that right?"

"You're giving me 2008 vibes, baby."

"Am I?"

"Mmmhmm."

"Is it because we met in the gym?" He leaned into me, weighing me down deliciously. I could feel one of his hands smooth along the curve of my hip.

"Maybe," I giggled.

"Or...could it be that you're trying to seduce me into canceling my birthday trip, so you can go to your little show and prance around the stage?" Keith's eyes darkened, no longer flirtatious and playful, but angry and accusing. He pulled away in frustration, tossing his hands in the air, "My God, Marlow! I can't believe what runs through your head half the time! You think I'm really that easy? That gullible? I know about you trying to distract me so I can agree to letting you dance."

"What are you talking about?"

"You know EXACTLY what I'm talking about. Your phone butt-dialed me earlier, and I heard you and Monica talking."

I swallowed the lump in my throat and the sound was harsh and loud.

Keith looked down on me with disappointment. "I know Monica and Tatyana are your girls, but sometimes I wonder how stupid you must be to follow their advice! Keep listening to them and they're going to make you lose this marriage. Watch."

In an instant, the corners of my eyes drew together tightly and my lips twitched. "Did you just call me 'stupid'?"

"You're not stupid, and you KNOW what I meant by that. I said..."

"No, don't try to sweeten it up! You called me stupid, Keith! Maybe you HAVE lost your mind." I drew my hand back and hit him with the heel of my palm, my voice shaky and disbelieving. I felt like another entity was occupying my body as my fingers trembled. "You've never disrespected me that way before, and I won't let you do it now!"

"Marlow, are you serious right now?" He moved his jaw around in irritation, and I could spot the redness that appeared from my heavy hand. "You're turning this around? It's your fault I said it in the first place! You're the one who—"

"And THERE you go! *There* it is!" I suddenly felt cold and unattractive under his stare. I began to clap theatrically, my lips twisting into a wicked smile, "There you go blaming me as usual! You can never take accountability for yourself, can you? It's always my fault, isn't it?"

"Of course it's all your fault," he chuckled bitterly, sounding like a movie villain. I hated the sound. "We wouldn't be in this mess if you hadn't brought up divorce talk, MARLOW! So think of that the next time you question anything else. It was YOU who gave up on us first. It was YOU who decided nothing else would work in our marriage, and it was YOU who threw in the towel first. You did! YOU did! YOU... DID!"

Keith's screams were unlike anything I'd heard before, filled with a whole lot of pain and disappointment. His eyes and voice were raw, piercing my soul and begging my heartstrings to break. I was the one who started this whirlwind, he was right—but it wasn't like he wasn't in agreement. He wanted the divorce just as much as I did.

"Like I said, you can never...EVER...just accept that you're not the perfect man I married. You do your dirt, too. You make your mistakes too. But it's only me, right?"

Swallowing back the shakiness in my throat was one of the hardest things I had to do, to keep from bursting into tears and wailing like a child. I thought back to Keith's brush with infidelity a couple years back.

He had hired an attractive secretary because of her resume, but too many late nights of work and late hours of swapping relationship and marital advice had proven too much for them to handle. Keith admitted to being attracted to the woman, but not actually following through when she made passes at him. He took action before the destruction, and had the woman transferred to another department before I got involved.

His time with her could have ruined our marriage, but I was thankful for his self-control and for realizing what path he was headed down.

"I swear to God you better not bring up that stuff with Nyomie. You hold that over my head like I slept with the woman. You act like I cheated on you." Keith rubbed his bruised face in frustration, practically foaming at the mouth.

"You said it, I didn't." I shrugged nonchalantly, though my blood and emotions were bubbling over and out of control. If we didn't switch subjects, cool down, or walk away from one another *soon*, I wasn't sure what was going to happen or what I was going to do. I didn't trust myself not to hit him again. He was pushing all the right buttons tonight.

We were so caught up in our deep breathing, finger pointing and blaming, that I didn't hear the collective weeps of our children. All three were huddled together at the top of the stairs, clutching onto the spiral railing, and looking down at us.

I couldn't tear my eyes from Keith, as we looked on at each other in disgust. Finally, he brushed past me, and took the stairs two at a time, scooping up Shalom, and then ushering David and Harlee to their bedrooms with a soothing voice. Embarrassed, fed up, and utterly helpless, I slid down the wall and wept quietly into my hands.

# CHAPTER 3: MARLOW

The yoga instructor's voice rang out soothingly around the 900-square foot studio, "Let's stretch out our legs, ladies, as we bring our heart rates down. Try to reach as far as you can to the ground...touch your toes if you must with your fingertips. Good, good. Deep breaths. In...out. In...out.

I inhaled deeply as I bent at the waist and extended my arms as far as they could reach. I was an athlete and dancer by nature, so the flexibility was no issue. Yet, I still slightly stumbled onto my knees, unable to keep my balance because of my lack of sleep and inability to focus on the yoga instructor.

My eyes were on her deep green stretch pants and the neon yellow logo at the corner of her hip, while my mind was on my argument with Keith, days ago. I still couldn't believe how volatile I'd gotten, no matter how angry he made me. I couldn't believe the unkind words we allowed to leave our lips. I certainly couldn't get the image of my crying children out of my mind. I never wanted them to see us arguing or yelling, let alone hitting and pushing one another.

It absolutely sickened me.

"Alright! Awesome class today, ladies. I'll be hosting one more session before I relocate to Michigan. Please come out for yoga and then refreshments afterward. The new instructor will be out next Saturday, if you're interested in continuing these classes. Single ladies, get this—it's a guy," she teased.

The small class erupted in catcalls, whistles and giggles.

Morgan was such a relatable, sweet soul. She was a promising dancer, who had suffered a career-ending toe injury three years ago, and retired from dancing, only to become a licensed massage therapist and part-time yoga instructor. It wasn't as exciting or glamorous as performing in front of thousands each night, but she loved it all the same.

Though several months pregnant, she could still bend and twist with the best of them. Her husband had accepted a new job in Detroit, so they were moving at the end of the month with his job and her dreams. Their leap of faith was inspiring to me.

The class of four exhausted women and two men slowly dispersed after all last-minute stretches were performed. We collectively wiped down our stations, sanitized our mats and hands, and then removed our masks for fresh air as we walked outside and piled into our respective vehicles.

The kids were home with Keith and my "mommy time" was coming to a close, but I had one last stop I needed to make. After picking up glazed donuts and cups of orange juice for the family, I stopped briefly in the drive-up teller line at the bank.

I filled out the necessary withdrawal slip, tucked my ID in the dispenser, and waited patiently for assistance.

"Hello, Mrs. Richmond, good to see you this morning. Any special way you would like this cash back?"

I smiled at the young girl through the window. "Big faces, please and thank you, Rashida. Oh, and love that hairstyle on you, girl!"

The transaction and small talk was over before it began, and as I drove away, I was careful to tuck the thick envelope deep down in my duffel bag.

When I made it home, Keith was outside, shirtless, in the neighbor's driveway. *Ugh.* Our young neighbor on the right was the perfect neighbor—he was quiet, minded his business, and he picked up behind his dog like any responsible pet owner should. The neighbors on our left were a sweet elderly couple with kind children and respectful grandchildren. Our neighbor across the street, however, was the complete opposite—she was single, messy, and showed off a little too much cleavage and legs for my liking. Why my husband was half naked and entertaining her was my only question as I backed into the driveway.

I called Harlee to the door to grab the donuts and juice from me, and then casually made my way over to the oblivious pair. Keith's back was to me, and Saige, the desperate ex-housewife, was hidden by a tree so I went undetected for a few minutes.

"Yeah, it's just a shame. People are still gathering and not treating this virus like the culprit it is. I mean seriously, almost a year into a pandemic, and people still don't wear masks properly! I fear for my life sometimes."

I rolled my eyes at her dramatization. She wanted to talk about social distancing, yet was in my husband's face.

"Right, you would think it'd be second nature by now, but there will always be people who don't believe the hype. I'm just thankful my wife and children, and I, haven't been personally affected by it. On all fronts, we're good."

"Yes, you are. I mean, I see the new truck your wife is rolling around in, and that big playground area you guys are installing for your children. It's inspiring to see."

"Thank you. Providing for my family is my number one priority." He shrugged.

"Your wife is a lucky, lucky woman." Saige took a step in his direction, wearing fitting lounge pants and a shirt that was a couple sizes too small.

Keith chuckled uncomfortably, rubbing the back of his neck. "No, *I'm* the blessed one. Seriously, she's the best."

I wasn't necessarily jealous at this exchange but I had to admit it felt good to hear Keith say those words. The confidence and assurance in his statement made me turn around and tiptoe back down the path to our home. Her next words stopped me.

"I thought I heard arguing the other night while I was walking my puppy. Is...everything okay? I've been married before, so I understand that..."

I whipped around and raised my voice, finishing her thought, "...that everybody's relationship and marriage is different, and completely not your business."

"Marlow! Hey," Keith jumped slightly, turned around, and greeted. I had to shake my head at his silly, deer-in-headlights expression. "When did you get home?"

"Just in time for me to see you over here talking with strangers. Your mother wouldn't approve and neither do I. Let's go...I picked up breakfast."

"Stop tripping. I was literally just helping her move some of these leaves."

"Nah. That's what her gardener is for. You know, the polite Hispanic teenager she underpays, or is it that she messes around with his father for compensation? Who knows?" I gave her a dirty look. "Come…on…Keith."

Saige looked surprised at my words, but didn't back down. "I didn't think it was a problem to ask for help, but next time I'll be sure to grab someone else. I didn't mean to disrespect you," she purred, clasping her hands in front of her, causing her chest to burst out of her shirt even more.

As Keith was halfway back down the driveway, I left her some final thoughts and did everything I could not to introduce my fist to her face. "Stay away from my family," I warned simply, spinning on my heel.

"With the way you two argue, I'd hardly think you two were a family, but…who am I to judge?" She continued, her voice sticky sweet yet dripping with sarcasm.

"You said it best. You hardly think." I batted my eyelashes with just as much innocence as she was giving off. "Like I said, stay away from my family, you pea brain wench. I'd hate to have to resort to violence."

"Using big words? I didn't think ballet dancers had a proper education other than learning how to plié, pirouette, and sauté."

I gave her another once-over, decided she wasn't worth the energy, and continued my trek back home. Her laugh that followed me made my skin crawl. Still, I only clenched my teeth and fists, and walked forward until I was standing inside of our foyer.

Keith was shrugging on his shirt and avoiding my stare.

"What was *that*?"

"Marlow, it wasn't what you thought. Don't start. I have a migraine."

"And I have an attitude that YOU caused by socializing with that low IQ, fake breasted, fake butt, botched surgery hussy."

His eyes widened at my insults, taking a step back.

I continued, unfazed, "I'm all ears. Because it looked exactly like what I thought it was."

"The whole exchange took five minutes. End of story."

"Uh, I'm not done reading this book. It's NOT the end! You KNOW how women like that operate, so why would you even go over there—shirtless and smiling in her face, at that? Not only that, but it's not even that warm outside so there was no reason to do that. And you know what else? She had the nerve to tell me she heard us arguing. Just what were y'all talking about before I walked up?"

"I didn't tell her anything! If she heard us arguing, it's because we were loud. What do you want me to tell you?"

"No, she was being nosey and fishing for information. I want you to tell me why you were over there."

Keith slammed his hands down on the countertop, rattling the knives in their wooden holder. "I literally ran over after playing basketball with David. My shirt was already off. I helped the woman move a pile of leaves from her lawn to the curb because she asked me. Not because I was flirting or wanted to upset you. I was just being a friendly neighbor."

"Yeah, you were friendly alright."

"If it makes you happy, I'm not talking to her ever again. Okay? Just—stop with the nagging."

"NAGGING? You call *this* nagging?"

"Shut uuuuup," Keith screamed, his head tossed back and his eyes tired. "My God! Just shut up!"

"Don't talk to me like that!"

"Then stop making up things to argue about! God! What happened to us, huh? Why can't we go a single day without yelling, arguing, and disagreeing now?"

I rounded the island, putting up pots and pans loudly. "Things have definitely changed. You would have never told me to shut up."

"Yeah, and when I met you, you weren't putting your hands on me either." He rubbed his face roughly a few times, and then growled lowly. "Marlow, I'm going to be very honest with you, baby. I—I don't like this."

"I don't like it either," I whispered, hoarse, and fighting back tears. The kids were awfully quiet and I feared that they were listening in on our discussion again.

"I know we've talked about it before, but maybe...just maybe it's about that time. The counseling, the therapy, the praying, the waiting...it's all leading us back to the same thing. We keep hurting each other and doing more damage than good. I refuse to disrespect or degrade you further. I love you too much, and I don't want to tarnish our friendship or foundation..."

There was a 'but' coming. I could feel it.

"...But if moving out or separating myself will help us, and help keep the peace, then maybe that's our next move. It's probably time we have that conversation with the kids." He sounded and looked defeated as our eyes finally locked. "It's time we really face the music, baby. We just...we just don't..."

Weakly, with a single tear falling from my eye, I finished his thought. "We just don't work anymore. I know, baby...I know..."

I was reminded of the money I had taken out of my account earlier and went to retrieve my purse. Keith was still leaning on the countertop with his head down and his lip tucked in thought, when I gave him the envelope.

"Here. This is my share of court costs, the divorce filing fee, and a little extra something, just in case. I haven't consulted with anyone, but I just want things to be cordial and quick. Whatever we do, please don't drag me through the mud or lose sight in how the kids feel in all of this."

Keith's eyes narrowed and glistened with tears. He didn't accept the money, or even give it another thought as he stepped back and walked away. I realized he hadn't expected my words or actions, and I had probably caught him off guard, but I knew that I didn't want to be like some of our mutual friends who were fighting tooth and nail to get money and material things from one another. I didn't want to be that couple.

That night, after dinner had been served, the children had been bathed and tucked in, and kisses and "I love yous" had been exchanged, I ran a warm shower. With the gentle slaps of water against my face and body, I sat in the corner of the tub, curled into a ball, where I cried harder than I had ever cried in my life. Everything was spiraling out of control; I was crying more than ever lately, and I could do absolutely nothing to stop or fix it.

Where did we go wrong?
Can't really even recall when things were right.
I'll decide what route to take,
Once we get over this fight.

We never used to argue or fuss;
You were always gentle and becoming.
Now I don't know the man you are,
or the woman I'm becoming.

Life is spiraling out of control;
Together, we've come undone.
Are these the kind of examples we're setting
for our daughters and son?

# CHAPTER 4: KEITH

*B*e *there in 10 mins. Sorry for the wait. Forgive me?*

I glanced up from the text message staring back at me, groaning inwardly. If there was one thing I hated, it was that I showed up on time or earlier than necessary to meetings and functions 99 percent of the time, yet others seemed to take my time and professionalism for granted. This time was no different as I ignored the subsequent smiley face and kissing face emojis that followed the text, and then tucked my phone in my pants pocket.

I was leaned against my car, one foot up against the driver's side door comfortably, and both hands tucked in my jacket pocket. My eyes, which were covered by dark shades, were on Shalom—just feet away—as she ran around a mostly empty playground. She was bundled up in a pink pea coat with cute little mittens, but the bulkiness didn't seem to bother her as she climbed up the mini stairs, slid down the slides, and even skipped along the sandbox edge.

Just behind the playground was one of the empty facilities I was potentially trying to buy, pending my meeting with an investor. This entire exchange had been setup behind Marlow's back, but I wouldn't dare sign any papers or make any further moves without her. No matter our marital status or the rockiness of our relationship, I would still include her in everything. She was my partner in all things and would always be.

An unfamiliar car pulled up just behind mine, and I paid the well-dressed woman no mind as she got out. Four or five children also climbed out and took off running to where Shalom played. I purposely stood up a little straighter to keep a better eye on her.

"Oh, she's fine. Relax. My son, nieces and nephew don't play rough," I heard to the side of me, closer than expected. To my surprise, the woman was settling inches away from me, and also leaning against my car.

"Uh, lady, don't do that. Don't lean on my vehicle," I warned, not exactly looking her in the face, but making sure she didn't prop her leg up. She had on knee-length boots that would be detrimental to my custom paint job.

The woman scoffed and pulled down her face covering to give me an incredulous look. It was Tatyana. "Ummm, excuse you? I ought to scratch your car up just for saying that. I guess Marlow was right; this pandemic has turned you mean."

For a moment, I laughed and rubbed my eyes free of fatigue. I hadn't slept properly in months, it seemed, and stress was at all-time high. "My bad, Taty. You threw me off."

"Obviously." She rolled her big doe eyes, and stood shoulder to shoulder with me. She blew out a hearty breath, the warmth disappearing out in front of her. "We were heading here anyway from our lunch date, but I knew I saw your distinctive plates, so I thought I'd stop by and say 'hello.'"

"How you been holdin' up?" I asked her, but my eyes stayed glued to my little girl. I had witnessed too many Lifetime movies where children had been abducted and wasn't taking any chances, even with other familiar faces around.

"We're good. Hubby's good and working hard; the children are excited to go back to their virtual learning and meet their new teachers soon. You?" She looked over and asked dryly, "Still got that stick up your butt?"

I nearly choked on my gum, sizing her up. "Excuse me?"

"Did I say something out of line? Oops." She shrugged and adjusted the mask over her mouth. Her eyes were darkened with disinterest. "I was just wondering if you'd come to your senses yet, that's all."

"Pertaining to what?"

"You know *exactly* what I'm referring to, and I'm sick of getting the text messages and calls from Marlow about the marriage that you guys worked so hard for. I know I'm not your momma, your pastor, and I definitely ain't Marlow, but take it from me—a married woman, with kids and someone who's had a similar journey like you guys—this back and forth and trying to separate won't work. You guys will be miserable without each other. The kids will suffer, and ultimately it'll be the worst decision of your lives. Please reconsider."

"Woooow." I shook my head and chuckled, but there was no joking or humor behind the sound. "So, what?

She talks about us to you ladies? And she gets on me for saying little things at the barbershop."

"No. Stop. Don't do that. We don't talk often, but it's obvious what's going on. Things haven't been the same for a while…and well, I heard an argument a few weeks back about you two possibly divorcing. Her phone butt-dials me quite often."

I could attest to that too.

Tatyana wrapped her arms around herself, bouncing slightly on the balls of her feet. "It's kept me up at night; I'm sure it's kept Monica up at night, and I KNOW Marlow has been stressed. Whether it stems from the different careers, her feeling stretched as a mother and wife, or simply just from you both FEELING like you've grown apart, I just feel like you haven't exhausted all options in order for a divorce to be the outcome."

"You're on the outside looking in though. We've done everything, Taty. I know you mean well, but seriously, we've come to a point where counseling, praying, and compromising just doesn't matter anymore. We promised to be friends through it all, and she'll always be the number one woman in my life, alongside our girls. People split all the time. Why is it so shocking that we've come to that point?"

"*Why*? You really have to ask?"

"We've been getting lectures from all sides and everybody seems to think it's all my fault."

"That's not necessarily true. We don't think it's any one person's fault, but I do know that even while we're talking about this subject, and your thoughts are on Marlow, your eyes have lit up like they always do. I know it's cold out, but your cheeks have reddened like they always do when you talk about her."

"God, you sound like a romance novel." I rolled my eyes.

"And you sound like you're in denial," she countered. "I'd be doing a disservice to both of my friends if I didn't point out these things, and didn't speak the truth. Call it what you want, but I know you love her still...just as she loves you still..."

"That's true, but..."

"But nothing. You've dedicated your life to each other; you've created a beautiful life TOGETHER, and you've created beautiful children TOGETHER. This union cannot fail. It just can't." Her eyes were on me intensely, slightly tearing up with the seriousness of her words, "Me and Monica's marriages literally shadow yours. We idolize you two, as badly as that sounds, and if you fail, we essentially fail."

"That's pressure I just don't want," I joked.

"You joke, but I'm nearly in tears, Keith. I can't tell you what to do, of course, but stay the course is all I'm saying. Never mind the rough patches because we all have them. It's part of life. It just happens that your rough patch has lasted a little longer than others. It's not grounds to just throw it all away. You don't want to regret this decision down the line when you could have been enjoying these years."

I had to admit, I was surprised to hear her words, but they were appreciated more than she knew. They warmed my heart and helped to put a piece of my shattered soul back in place, as crazy as it sounded. Of course, I knew our union was unique and special and God-sent, but the innocence and purity of it had been lost along the way. According to Tatyana, we could still get it back. The question was, with all the headaches I had given Marlow recently, would SHE want it back?

We had some work to do, certainly some talking to do, and I was determined to make things right after today. Hopefully she forgave me for my current endeavors…

As Tatyana pulled away from the quick hug she gave me, her eyes caught the approaching vehicle before I did. She gave me questioning eyes. "Expecting someone?"

I turned and admired the luxury vehicle as it rolled to a stop in front of mine. The front passenger door opened, and out stepped an older gentleman with salt and pepper hair, tiny glasses perched on the bridge of his nose, and a briefcase at his side. The back passenger door opened and there was Saige with a mink coat on, tall boots, and an icy white smile wrapped in her cherry red lips.

"I'm so sorry we're late! Thank you for waiting. I couldn't find the matching bracelet to my earrings, and ugh…it was just a hassle," she explained, and it wasn't until now that I realized how annoying her voice was. She sounded like something straight out of an animated television series.

"It's alright. I brought my daughter along so she could play around while I waited."

She nodded absently, tugging on the older guy's arm. "Well, let's get right into it. Keith, this is my father and investing partner, Marx Penny. Daddy, this is my neighbor, Keith Richmond, and the guy who wants to purchase your space for another health club."

"Athletic center," I corrected.

"It's all the same." She winked. Her eyes locked on Tatyana in confusion. "I didn't know we were entertaining other guests. And you are?"

"It's really none of your—" Tatyana began to say, but I nudged her with my elbow. She cleared her throat and kept quiet, causing Saige's eyebrows to raise in question.

"Saige, this is Tatyana, one of my wife's best friends. She's not part of the meeting today; we were just catching up while our children played together."

"We've met before actually," Tatyana spoke dryly, no longer as sweet as she had sounded with me. Her eyes gave Saige a once-over and then she widened her eyes in my direction as if to say, "what is going on?" I knew she had questions but now wasn't the time. I just hoped she didn't tell Marlow before I got the chance to tell her myself.

"Oh, you have? I don't recall your face." Saige extended her hand. "Church? Work?"

Tatyana feigned confusion of her own as I looked back and forth between the two. "Oh, no, you're right. I thought you were someone else. You favor one of the former prostitutes that joined my church a couple weeks back. She's since given her life to Christ." Tatyana leaned in close to Saige, her voice loud and clear and dripping with sarcasm, "Say, honey, do you accept Jesus Christ as your Savior?"

"TATY!" I whisper-yelled, shocked but also amused. It took everything in me not to fall over in laughter. Tatyana had always been witty and comical and just downright crazy. Plus, she was super protective over Marlow and I could appreciate that.

Saige looked flustered and offended as she stood upright and tugged her coat tighter around herself. "Ugh! Keith, are you trying to talk business or no? I don't have time for the shenanigans."

"Sorry about that." I mustered up the strength to wipe the smirk off of my face and motioned for her to follow me. "Taty, are you staying here for a while with the kids?"

She nodded, coolly leaning against my car again, and waving. "Go to your meeting. Be back in 30, though. The kids have dentist appointments at four."

"Will do—I owe you, girl!" I called out.

"Just consider what I said, and we're good!" she yelled back.

More than an hour later, Shalom and I were making our way into the house with takeout shrimp fried rice, egg rolls, and a 2-liter of the Richmond Family's favorite soda, grape. I had sent a text to Marlow, letting her know that I was bringing food home, but she didn't respond. I figured she had gotten tied up and that was okay. My wife was a busy woman, and had been holding everything down gracefully with no complaints.

The more time that passed since speaking with Tatyana, the more of an idiot I felt for giving Marlow such a hard time. I needed to make things up to her in a major way.

This was more than a flowers and candy type of job; I needed to prove to her that I still loved her and wanted to be with her. I needed to show her that I considered her feelings, and thought she was still just as special as the day we met. But in all my helplessness, I had no idea where to start picking up the pieces.

My smug, idiotic ways had finally caught up to me, and had now threatened the happiness and peace of the one person who loved me unconditionally.

Maybe, just maybe, my planned surprise would work out in time and salvage it all.

"Babe!" I called out. "We're home with food. Kids, come on down and get ready for dinner."

Harlee and David were prompt as they filed into the kitchen but Marlow was still nowhere to be found. I looked at my eldest children. "Where's Mom?"

"In a meeting."

"Oh, conference call?" I pulled out a stack of paper plates and handed them to Harlee. She shook her head and her long braids slapped the sides of her face gently.

"No, with a lawyer in the upstairs office. I can't remember his name."

That stopped me in my tracks. I paused as I scooped rice onto Shalom's plate, and put everything down. I instructed David to take over for me, while I wiped my hands quickly, and then jogged up the stairwell leading to our home office. Sure enough, as I rounded the corner, Marlow was leaving the office with a man in tow. He was dressed in a perfectly tailored navy suit and looked alarmed as our eyes met.

"Mr. Richmond, good evening." He presented me with his short, thick hand to shake.

"It'll be even better when you leave so I can have dinner with my wife. Who are *you?*" I felt an uneasiness in the pit of my stomach. He carried a briefcase, and a manila folder filled with paperwork was tucked under that same arm.

Marlow butted in this time and stood between us. She waved a glossy business card in my face and smiled. "You're not the only one setting up secret meetings," she said simply.

Then, she turned to the shorter man. "So good speaking with you again, Darren. We will be in touch. Would you mind seeing yourself out while I speak with him?"

"You bet. Mr. Richmond, enjoy your evening." The attorney extended his hand for a second time, and then chuckled when I only stared at it. "Yeah. I should've expected that."

"Don't come to my house again. I may not be so patient next time." I stared at his back in warning.

"I'll remember that," the guy called out and it was evident by his laugh that he didn't take me seriously. I watched his retreating form until he left out of the front door.

My eyes swung over to Marlow where she moved to go back in the room.

"Yo, like for real...what was *that*? Why was he here? We didn't agree to start hiring attorneys and we definitely aren't going to start bringing people over to the house. How could you bring that around the kids, Marlow?"

"Oh, you be quiet!" she hissed. "Let's not talk about bringing people around our kids. Worry about not prancing around in plain sight with the neighborhood help."

"*What?*"

"You…Saige…downtown! Get the picture? Because I got one!" She fished around in her pocket for her phone, scrolled through it for a few moments, and then turned it towards me.

I closed my eyes in frustration. "*Taty*," I hissed.

"Tatyana didn't send me anything. This is from my hairdresser. Just imagine, if *she* saw you, who else could have possibly seen you? What were you two doing down there?"

For a moment, all I could do was stare and hate myself. It made me feel two feet tall to think of what Marlow was feeling, after receiving the image of me and Saige having lunch together, especially after I had promised not to speak to the woman ever again.

The picture showed two people comfortably talking and cozy together in a booth, yet we were literally talking business the entire time. There was no way I could fix this up.

Marlow had been so broken that she had contacted a divorce attorney the same day. Either that, or a meeting had already been planned behind my back. Whatever the case, she was finally fed up and my actions had only further justified her decision to leave me. That thought killed me. "Baby, I—I can't say."

Marlow pressed her lips together, nodded a few times, and then backed away. "Right. Figures. Goodnight, Keith."

As much as I wanted to tell her what was going on, I couldn't. It would ruin everything I was trying to do. But as she slammed the door on me and I joined my confused children back in the kitchen, I knew my own foolishness had ruined us. I didn't need anybody's help in looking idiotic this time.

# CHAPTER 5: KEITH

"Mr. Richmond, you have a call on line two." I looked over from my composition notebook, nodding once to my secretary's whispered words. I had been scribbling notes down, and half paying attention to the guest lecturer speaking at the front of the room to the audience of 15 masked men and women.

As an entrepreneur and the CEO of three lucrative athletic centers around the state, and a handful of clients needing my custom personal training services at the drop of a dime, it was not uncommon to be in such an intense meeting so early in the morning. I was happy for the interruption; though, I wondered who could be calling me. As quietly as possible, I scooted away from the table, gathered my belongings, and speed-walked out of the conference room.

My office was just a few feet away, so after entering and closing the door, I settled behind my desk and picked up the phone receiver. I pressed '2' and waited a few beats.

"Good after—*er*, morning. Keith Richmond speaking. How may I help you?"

The sun felt heavenly today, as it shone brightly, and made the day substantially warmer than its below 30-degree temperatures. I couldn't believe Durham was getting slammed with so much wintry weather lately, and Thanksgiving hadn't even shown its face. My eyes were locked on the imagery beyond the seventh-floor window, as I leaned back and prepared to speak with a potential partner or client.

"Keith. Hey, man...I hope I didn't catch you at a bad time."

It was my accountant, Tim.

"Hey, how you doing, bro?" He sounded uneasy, so I just had to ask. "You okay?"

"No complaints over this way, man. Just trying to get through the workweek, you know?" He chuckled lightly and then cleared his throat. "Again, I'm sorry for the random midmorning call, but there was some activity on your account that I figured you should be aware of. I was preparing your monthly budgeting reports, and maybe you already know this, but...your credit card was maxed out."

"*Maxed out?*" I repeated. "Tim, that card has almost $4,500 on it. It's an emergency card, and neither I nor Marlow have had an emergency recently. It's got to be fraud."

"Not necessarily. Hear me out." He read off the amount and I could tell he was clicking through some on-screen information by the frequent *taps* on his end. "I looked up where the withdrawal came from and it's a place you guys frequent often. The getaway spot in Florida."

"The Alcove?"

"That's it. You mean to tell me you have no recollection of this? You didn't book the vacation?"

"No," I spoke through gritted teeth, clutching the phone. My knuckles became sore and pale as I tightened my grip. "It's got to be Marlow's doing. She's the only one with access to the card."

"Look, I'm sorry if I just ruined some sort of surprise that she may have set up for you, but it was worth noting. These days, you can never be too sure about anything."

"Yeah, yeah." My answer was inattentive and quiet.

"Do me a favor; once you find out it was Marlow, give me a call back. I'll be in the office for a few more hours."

"Will do. Thanks for calling and checking in, Tim. I appreciate you."

"You bet. Take care, bro."

As I set the receiver down, I literally felt my blood boil from the inside out. My expression hardened to the point of pain, and my fingers drummed in a monotonous manner as I gathered my thoughts. Why in the world my wife would spend almost three times our mortgage for a weekend vacation was beyond me. I was especially annoyed because she had not okayed it with me. Even though we were better off than most people, we were still on a "rich man's budget" these days with the uncertainty of the economy. This frivolous charge was a step in the wrong direction.

She was getting back at me for my meeting with Saige; that was the only conclusion. But this was nonsense. She was going about it in the wrong way.

I thought about her schedule for the day and knew she was in her 90-minute yoga and meditation class downtown. The studio was about 11 minutes away, so instead of calling her, I made an effort to pay her a visit. I had to show her just how upset I was, and catching her off guard, in person, would allow us to have a more productive conversation.

At least I hoped it went down that way...

When I pulled into the parking lot of the six-store shopping center, I saw women filing out of the class. Some were chatting—their mouths and expressions hidden behind their masks. Others were walking alone, clutching yoga mats and bottled waters. Then there was my wife.

She was the only woman chatting with a man. They made up the rear of the group, walking closely, and laughing like old friends. She didn't have on a face cover, and neither did the man beside her. He was unfamiliar yet average looking—not overly muscular, with low cut hair, flirtatious eyes, and not so good intentions.

"She gets pissed at me for talking to our neighbor, but she's smiling in this clown's face?" I sat for a few moments, watching them laugh and lean into each other. I felt a twist in my gut, a tug that told me not only was I jealous, but I was angrier than I'd ever been in awhile.

I unbuckled my seatbelt and slid out of the car in what seemed like one fluid motion. I slammed the door closed and pocketed my keys. I didn't bother to put a mask on or even keep my distance as I walked right up to the two and stood nearly chest to chin with my wife. She glanced up, with tears of laughter in her eyes, and then sobered up quickly.

"Keith? What are you...?"

"Get in the car." I peered down at her, but then my eyes slowly slid over to the strange man, looking on.

"I drove my car, remember? Keith, what are you doing here? What's going on? Something happened with one of the kids?"

"They're safe and sound and doing what they should be doing. I wish I could say the same about you." I turned my cap to the back of my head, licking my lips. "Get in the car, 'Low."

"Why would I get in your car if I drove? I don't get it. What's wrong? You knew I was at yoga."

"Yeah, with other women. I didn't know you and Taye Diggs would be hugged up when I got here." I motioned to the guy, as he chuckled and stepped forward.

"Who are you? Marlow, who is he? Do I need to call security?"

"'Cause we all know you need a man to save you from another man, right?" I shook my head and laughed at his expression. "Clown. Marlow, let me talk to you for a minute...ALONE."

She stood there for a second in her navy stretch pants, black flats, and navy and gold sports bra. An unzipped, lightweight jacket covered her arms. I didn't remember her leaving the house that way, but figured none of the women had left their homes in the tight fitting, midriff-baring clothing.

Finally, Marlow turned to the guy. "I'm so sorry for my husband. He's been under a lot of stress lately, and acting strangely. Thank you for today. It was much needed, and it was so good to see you again."

The two hugged, and the wannabe bodybuilder took off in the opposite direction. Marlow watched him go with a smile before she looked at me with a crazed look in her eye.

"Taye Diggs? *Really?* You want to play the big guy now and act a fool in front of people—*really?*" She swung her neck as she spoke. Her hair, that was braided halo-style, glistened with glitter, or maybe it was sweat. "I don't know who you are anymore. I really don't."

"Me?" I took a step back. "What's up with you and that guy? You're the only woman leaving an all-female yoga class with some random guy, hugging it up and laughing like old lovers. What was I supposed to think?"

"You're supposed to trust your wife and carry on like a civilized Christian man. That's an old friend, who used to dance with me back in the day. He's married to a GUY, and they have three beautiful foster children. But you didn't know that. Instead, you embarrassed him. You embarrassed me, and you embarrassed yourself. That wasn't cool, Keith. I can't believe you." She placed her yoga mat on the ground upright, leaning onto it. "What are you even doing here and not at work?"

It was like a flood hit me. Suddenly, my anger for what had transpired didn't seem as bad. The information that the accountant gave me came back and took my irritation to another level.

"What did you spend over $4,000 on, Marlow? Tim called me and said a trip to The Alcove was booked."

"What? *The Alcove*? We haven't been there in years." She genuinely looked shocked. "I didn't book a trip. Are you kidding me? I wouldn't do something like that unless we've talked about it first. You know that."

"I *don't* know that, which is why I'm asking you. I gave that card to you for emergencies only. It shouldn't have gone to some weekend getaway, or whatever you were trying to do. I don't understand your thinking sometimes."

"And I don't understand your comprehension abilities." She crossed her arms under her chest. "I didn't use the card. In fact, I haven't used the card, since we bought that $200 mattress for Shalom, months ago. Oh, and some groceries here and there because I didn't have cash."

"Where's the card now?"

"In my wallet."

"Let me see it."

"Let's talk about this at home. I'm not going through this with you out in the middle of a parking lot, Keith." She rolled her eyes and continued to gather her belongings. "I'll meet you at home."

"I'm going back to work."

"Whatever!"

"Yeah." I watched her strut off, unbothered and unfazed, "You just better make sure you call and cancel by the time I get off."

By six that evening, after the most stressful, irritating workday of my career, I called Marlow to see if she'd cancelled her spur of the moment getaway. She didn't answer, as I half suspected so I sped the entire way home to confront her. I was liable to do or say anything with the anger pumping through my veins, so I had to say a quick prayer of patience and peace.

That probably wasn't the smartest decision because the moment I entered our home, Marlow was in my face, pointing her finger, and accusing me of cheating.

She had to be referring to a math quiz back in the day. Infidelity was not my thing—it never had been and never would be. Well, except that one time...but that really wasn't cheating.

"Yo, calm down! What are you talking about? What's going on?"

Marlow had a face full of tears, melting foundation, and running mascara. Though still beautiful beneath the gunk, it was still alarming to witness. What would make her accuse me of such a sin?

She stepped back only slightly, wiping the back of her hand across her face, and holding a note in the other. She hiccupped and I suddenly saw Harlee and Shalom in the childlike expression.

"Baby, what are you fussing at me for? Why are you crying and upset?" I was calmer this time in my questions, seeking to understand and not yell.

"That...that stank social media model wannabe across the street came over and said you left some stuff at her home. When were you inside of her house, Keith? Why does she have your gym bag, and your clothes, and...and your toiletries? Huh? Answer me!" Marlow had a crazed look in her eye, something I could only attribute to the confusion and anger she felt.

I was in the same boat because I had no idea what she was talking about.

"I wasn't over that woman's house. How about trusting your man and knowing I wouldn't do that to you, to us, or the kids. Why did she have my bag?"

"Keith, you tell ME!"

"She's lying," I said simply, shrugging. "And I'm not entertaining any other conversation after tonight, other than asking her why she felt the need to stir up some drama with you."

"You're not asking her anything. I'm the only one communicating with her from here on out."

"Fine, whatever. Do what you gotta do, but baby, I don't know how she got my bag. I wasn't over there."

Marlow stared at me, unmoving, for several pregnancy pauses. It was like she was looking into my soul, something only she could do successfully. When she finally blinked and looked away, I saw the glimmer of disappointment and frustration disappear.

"I believe you," she said quietly, sniffling. "But any communication with her ceases. TODAY. Indefinitely."

"Done," I told my wife.

Marlow turned and balled the note up in one hand, and threw it away, all in a single motion. I was distracted briefly by the swing of her hips in her butt-eating satin shorts, before I shook my head to clear my thoughts. Wait a minute—I had some concerns of my own.

"Marlow, hold up. What happened with the reservations? Did you cancel everything?"

"I'm not talking about this with you, Keith. Not now, not ever. I didn't make the reservations and I'm not going back and forth with you about it. If you don't believe me, then I can't help you."

"Then who charged $4,056.32 to our emergency credit card—which, might I add, has been in your purse since the thing was shipped to our house. Marlow, stop walking away when I'm talking to you."

"I made it clear we were done with this conversation."

"But I'm not!"

"Mom? Dad?"

# CHAPTER 6: MARLOW

Distracted, I looked over at David as he stepped up cautiously, looking back and forth between us.

"I've got something to tell you..."

"Baby, me and Daddy just need to talk really quick. I promise we will be right up, okay? Five minutes." I forced a smile, hating the toxicity we were bringing to our home lately. Between the arguments, tension and fussing, I was growing more and more tired. I could only imagine the effect it had on the rest of the house.

Shalom and Harlee also stood feet away, holding hands, and looking concerned. I turned to Keith and we both agreed silently on one thing. We had to get our stuff together; this wasn't the environment we wanted to set for our babies.

"We're okay, kids. We just got really excited over some things but Daddy and I are okay. You hear me? We'll be okay," I promised, and somehow I hoped that reassurance for the kids would console me, also. Truth be told, I wasn't okay—WE weren't okay—and the outcome of things turning out okay didn't look promising either. I wouldn't dare share or express that with my kids.

"Yeah, me and Mom love you guys and we don't ever want you three to forget that. You guys didn't do anything wrong, you hear me?"

They nodded in unison, favoring one another. I couldn't help but to smile at our creations, our young king and young queens in the making. All three were superstar scholars, with beautiful and fresh imaginations, creativity out of this world, and hearts of compassion. I knew each of them would get into great colleges someday, marry great like-minded spouses, and make decisions we all could be proud of.

If we had not done anything else correctly, we had definitely made and raised awesome human beings.

"As a matter of fact, guys, we...um, we have to talk to you about something important. Let's go to the family room," Keith suggested, his voice gentle with seriousness.

Harlee swallowed hard as she led the family down the hall and to the cozy room we had conducted many important discussions like moving to a new school district, talks of racism and how our skin color shouldn't determine how we're treated, how to dial 911 for emergencies, and now...apparently, how divorce would look for the Richmond Family. The thought killed a piece of my soul.

"Never in a million years," I whispered, hoping God somehow sent the strength and words to say.

I pulled Shalom onto my lap, as Harlee sat a couple feet away from me, and Keith continued to stand at the head of the table. David leaned into the doorframe, twisting his fingers in nervousness, and made no move to join us at the table.

He was never good with serious talks, and it dawned on me that he had taken after his father in that sense. Every man I'd ever known seemed to shut down when it came to expressing himself, but I wanted differently for David. I was raising him to show his emotions, speak his mind, and be an effective communicator.

"Baby, come sit down. Once your dad and I are finished, we can all go around and share how we're feeling," I coaxed him.

His eyes watered behind his glasses. I could see them glistening from where I sat. He took off his frames in frustration, crying out, "It's all my fault!"

"What's your fault? You didn't do anything wrong, son. Come here."

"I did. I caused all of this," he motioned with his hands, "I'm the reason you argue all the time and hate each other. I'm the reason you're mad at each other. I'm—I'm the reason you're going to separate!" He screamed the last part, as a flood of emotion overtook him.

"It's not your fault, baby," I assured him.

We watched him slide down the doorframe in slow motion, it seemed, with his eyes locked on the ceiling, and his glasses clutched in his hands.

"Please don't break up! Please don't get a divorce! Please! I'll make it right."

My eyes locked on Keith's in confusion. David was blaming himself, but for what? Our children were the ones suffering in this, yet David cried with the weight of the world on his young shoulders.

"Son, come here," Keith called out. "Mom and I don't blame you for anything."

"That's 'cause you don't know what I did," he explained, hiccupping, "It was me!"

"What was you? What happened?"

"Dad, I'm the one who took the credit card from Momma's purse when she wasn't looking. I went on the travel website you always use and booked a trip at the place you guys like to visit. I thought it would make you happy. I thought by booking a vacation, it would make you smile and stop arguing, but I made things worse."

Keith froze in place and I closed my eyes completely, letting it all soak in. Shalom eventually squirmed from my arms, and I didn't realize I had been squeezing her until she whimpered. Before either of us could respond, David continued coming clean.

"And Momma, I was the one with Dad's gym bag. I needed it to carry my water bottle and ball. I took it when I went to play basketball with Miss Saige's nephew. I didn't mean to leave it over there, but she brought it over today and made it seem like Dad was over. It was me...all me! I'm sorry!" David was bawling by now, unable to move or do anything else but cry.

Keith stared at me, silently consulting with me, but I couldn't quite meet his eyes.

I didn't feel upset with my son at all; as a child, I had witnessed my parents go through a divorce and it wasn't fun. I still grew sad from time and time when I thought of the slander, anger, and lifelong pettiness that came with my parents' separation.

To this day, nothing had ever been the same, so I could only imagine how he felt. His actions hadn't been the wisest, but he was only eight.

"Kids, let me tell you something. There is nothing...NOTHING you can do to make me or your mom stop loving you...or stop loving each other."

My breath caught in my throat as I listened to Keith take charge of the room.

"David, you made a mistake. It's okay. I make them too, and for as long as we're on this earth, we will continue to make mistakes because nobody is perfect. That's no reason to beat yourself up or blame yourself for the way we've been acting around here. Me and Mom just have some things to work out."

"So are you getting a divorce?" It was Harlee this time, speaking through thick, crocodile tears. "My friends all look up to you, and they think we're the perfect family, but lately, I just don't know anymore. I hate when you two scream at each other," she added.

"Me too," Shalom whined. "Please don't be angry anymore."

My chest felt heavy as I listened to our children express themselves. I felt guilty that I had contributed to the added stress in our household.

"No, Harlee. To answer your question, baby girl," Keith began to say, "Yes, we're staying together. We won't be getting a divorce, and I'm sorry you felt that way. In fact,

I'm going to call The Alcove, and we're going to go on that family trip and let God handle the rest. It's been a long, crazy year, but I think we all could use this time away. What do you say?"

The kids, of course, were down for any kind of travelling. I still wasn't sure about what was happening, but I felt overwhelmed. I also trusted him and if he felt this trip was needed, then I was willing to go wherever he led us. I could feel Keith's eyes on me as I turned and headed to our bedroom without another word. I didn't stop walking until I reached the bathroom where I ran a hot bubble bath.

Hours seemed to have passed before I heard him stroll through our bedroom and up to the tub I'd been submerged in. Bubbles tickled my chin, and sweat beads formed along my hairline from the heat of the water. This bath was everything I needed, but as our eyes connected, I knew it would be short-lived.

"Look, I'm sorry for putting you on the spot that way. I couldn't really say what I wanted to say, but I know—for the sake of the kids—we, at least, owe them this family trip. Who knows when we'll be all together again like this?"

I shrugged silently.

"Nothing to say?"

I shook my head. "There's nothing more to be said. I stand with you, and now I just want to relax. I don't want to cry or argue or stress anymore. The fact that our five-year-old picked up on how angry we've been tells me I have some serious soul-searching to do. That...cannot happen again. Our children are literally suffering."

"Yeah. That tore me up, too," he admitted. "Has it really gotten that bad?"

Keith pulled his pants up slightly by the crotch and sat down on the edge of the tub. He kept his eyes on the wall ahead of him, but his body was angled towards me. "Do I really stress you out that much?"

I sank down even further, sighing, and blowing light pink suds in the process, "It's not *you*...per se. It's the wondering what's next; it's the disagreements over little things. It's the changes around here. We never used to argue, or get angry with one another. We were never mean to one another. To go from it not happening at all, to it happening all the time is draining."

He nodded slowly, thoughtfully, bringing his eyes to meet mine. I was taken aback by the expression on his face, the way he bit down on his lip in wonder, and the tears forming in his brilliant eyes.

"When did things go left? When did we...grow apart?"

"I—I don't know."

"We used to slow dance in the middle of the living room. Just two young kids in love, with nothing better to do than entertain ourselves, and have fun."

I smiled, reminiscing. "You were a terrible slow dancer, but I also felt so safe in your arms."

Keith returned my smile, and then it slowly faded. "When did our hearts no longer align, babe? I'm not placing the blame on either of us, but...I just have to know. We made promises before God and our family, with the intentions to be together forever. As far as I was concerned, I was stuck wit'chu for eternity. What...changed?" He genuinely looked concerned.

"Keith, I..."

"I still love you, Marlow."

I could not break our stare if I tried, sinking even further into the slippery ivory. By now, my lips were being kissed by the warm water. Despite the chaotic night, I felt relaxed. I felt like I was floating. I felt good. I felt... peace, as his words of affection permeated the atmosphere and slid over me like a blanket.

My heart could only repeat not only what it knew, but what it also felt, "I still love you too, Keith. I always will."

He closed his eyes briefly, a smile threatening to disfigure his lips, but he never broke. He opened them back up and for the first time in a long time, I saw lust. I saw intrigue, desire and want.

"We would make love like...rabbits, once upon a time."

"Stop it," I hissed.

"It's true." He shrugged, his tone flirtatious and low. "I stayed on fire for you, and even though we hardly ever do it these days, that fire has never been snuffed out. You're still the sexiest and most beautiful woman in the world to me."

With our eyes still locked, I watched as my husband's warm hand slid into the sea of bubbles. His arm disappeared almost until the curve of his elbow, and I closed my eyes when his hand connected with my inner thigh. From there, he explored my body as though it were the first time.

"*Keith*..." His name left my voice box as a moan.

"Shhh, it's been so long, baby. Just let me take care of you tonight. Give me that. Please. We can figure out everything else as it comes. For tonight, you need me, and I definitely need you."

"Keith, please." Truthfully, I wanted this just as badly as he wanted it, and it confused me. I thought that any lingering attraction for him had dissipated, somewhere lost in the qualms of why we married.

"Come here, baby," he whispered, and the huskiness of his request overtook me.

His eyes, his body language, and his voice were pointing to one thing as his actions from previous days spoke another. We always said things we didn't mean when we were angry. Plus, who was I to deny him? He was still my husband regardless, and if there was one thing the older mothers had taught me at church, it was to never deny your husband intimacy, unless of course you just weren't up for it or menstruating. Like I said, I wanted this just as badly as he did.

He helped me to a stand, dried me off, and then extended his arm so that I could climb out of the tub. With just a towel, mixed emotions, and wild thoughts, I followed him to our bedroom where he assured me the kids were all ready for bed and put away for the night.

We needed to talk—first with our lovemaking, and then verbally.

I moved to take my towel off, but didn't get the chance. Keith was gentle as he spun me around and yanked me by the towel knot. I slammed into his chest with a small yelp, seconds before my mouth was covered in his. We stumbled through the bedroom, clawing at one another, and half-tripping on the strewn garments we'd just discarded.

My back slammed into the wall, and for a moment I had to blink away my surprise. He left me there to grab a bottle of moisturizer, and then proceeded to rub the thick, scented cream over every inch of my skin. Softly, he chased each rub with a kiss here, nibble there. Goodness—I'd missed this. I'd missed HIM.

Keith worked his way up my body again, kissing me senselessly until I had to push against his shoulders to allow me time to breathe. I soon felt the feel of the bed behind the backs of my legs, and I went down shortly after. Keith climbed on top of me with a chuckle. "You okay?" he whispered, not missing a beat between kisses and caresses.

I nodded, still shocked that we were genuinely showing affection to one another, and embraced the lust I felt for him. His warmth and eagerness excited me more. We rolled around the oversized bed, a tangle of limbs and duet of moans, until finally, he settled on me deliciously and held my wrists down.

Keith buried his head in my neck and began a trail of sweet kisses to the curve of my breasts. He had me right where he wanted me—a heap of body butter, curves, and erratic breathing, and I was submissive to whatever he wanted of me.

Our pregame warm-up was rushed yet passionate, coupled with "I love yous" and "I'm sorrys." His hands were heavy against my body, molding against my warm skin, as his short fingernails created patterns along my scalp. I wasn't into the hair pulling, and hadn't been probably since the kids were born, but tonight it seemed we were revisiting all of our old tricks in the bedroom.

"Are you sure?"

He paused to cup the side of my face. "You talk as if we aren't married. I want it. I want YOU," he made clear. "Don't you?"

"Yes."

"Say no more, baby."

Our lovemaking was reminiscent of our wedding night, so many moons ago. We were in our late 20s all over again—energetic, passionate and intense. We spoke only to give a moan of approval, or quick instructions for deeper, harder pleasure. Our bodies and minds, for the first time in a long time, were in sync. I wanted nothing more than to please him, and he seemed to want to prove to me a lot tonight. It felt good. THIS felt good.

Together, we were good, and we had no reason to be so unkind and so curt with one another. As we both released months of sexual frustration together—our eyes lowered but locked, and our bodies pressed tightly as one—I knew I could never divorce or leave him.

That just wasn't in our stars.

# EPILOGUE: MARLOW

*Weeks later...*

I rolled over to warm sun rays kissing my forehead from the slightly opened blinds. Usually, I didn't sleep in so long or so deeply, but the night's extracurricular activities explained the need for an extra hour of snoring, cuddling, and sighing contently. The thought of consummating our renewed marriage over the last couple of weeks brought a smile to my face.

In the process of chuckling and reliving Keith's affection, I caught a whiff of bacon, something with bell peppers...and cinnamon rolls. Not only was my husband literally rocking my world every night, but he was also regularly cooking up something good for our stomachs the morning after. Ha. The morning after.

It still sounded funny when I thought of how quickly things had switched around for the better.

126

The reality of it all overwhelmed me, as I sat there nuzzling further in the sheets, squeezing my legs together, and biting down on my lip. We were some of the "lucky" ones. It didn't take long, drawn-out therapy sessions to get to this point or actually signing the divorce papers like so many of our relatives and friends. It didn't take the nasty breakup and splitting up of our children for some sense to be knocked into us. Hope came in the form of a mischievous yet loving human being—our son. After all, reconciliation was possible because of the antics of David. His actions—though costly—allowed us to finally face the music.

"Thank You, God." My body was deliciously sore and my eyes wrinkled in the corners as I smiled with pleasure. I was sure I looked like a crazy person, just smiling hard, with my eyes closed, while stretching my limbs gingerly from left to right.

The day's agenda was a lengthy one. There was motherly duties, wifely duties, career woman duties, and "me time" duties to be completed, but for now, I just needed relaxation and a moment to bask in what was to come.

Apparently, the universe thought otherwise as I was suddenly smacked on the side of the leg. The warm sheets were snatched off of my body, a sprinkle of liquid hit my face, and all too familiar giggles could be deciphered through the shock.

"Oh my...I know that's not you, Harlee..." I fought to catch my breath and sort through my thoughts. "David...Shalom...*KEITH*! WHAT IN THE WORLD?"

"Rise and shine, you...skank."

*Hold up*. I blinked a few times to make sure my eyes weren't deceiving me. Monica and Tatyana looked on with knowing grins, playful eyes, and crossed arms. "Mmmhmmm," they chorused.

"Clearly, she got some," Monica purred. "The room just smells of sex."

"...and bacon. *Oooooh*, I wonder if he made enough for us?" Tatyana trailed off when Monica nudged her.

"Ummm, HELLO? What are y'all doing here? And why'd you splash water on me? That was COLD!" I struggled to free myself from the tangle of cotton sheets and a twisted satin gown. In the process, my chest became exposed a few times, and if it were anyone else, I would have been embarrassed. These ladies had been in the delivery room with me as I pushed out Shalom, and they were my "quick change" partners on tour, so I had nothing to hide.

"We're here to say our goodbyes before we hit the road with the crew. We know you won't be joining us. Keith already gave us the rundown," Tatyana explained.

"Yeah…yeah…but that still doesn't explain the water."

"You were smiling like a Cheshire cat. We had to wake you somehow," Monica teased.

I rolled my eyes. "Some friends you are."

"You love us."

"Unfortunately, I do more than I care to admit. Safe travels and please check in when you can." I finally stood up, blanket-free and with a clearer mind. "I'm gonna miss you two, but I know you'll text and video call me every chance you get. Just don't have too much fun without me. Awww," I pretended to pout and whine.

"That's not even possible, honey. Aww, come here. Bring it in…Group hug!"

"Group hug! We love you." Monica kissed my cheek, and if I didn't know them any better, I would have dismissed any physical contact. But I was aware that the ladies had to undergo extensive testing to ensure they were safe to travel and tour. "You know you're the backbone of this group and the tour, and you'll be sorely missed," she added.

Even though their words were sincere, neither woman truly looked upset or bothered that I was staying behind. *Heffas.*

"Keith told us you'll be going on a trip of your own to celebrate his birthday and get one more family trip in before he opens up his fourth athletic center and all that other good stuff, so you have a nice time as well. I'm glad to see things coming together again for you guys," Tatyana mused sincerely.

"I'm glad too. It was a major test and a situation I don't want to ever be in again with us going behind each other's backs, bringing up divorce, arguing and fussing, and…" I shook my head free of the thoughts. "It's a new day and a new beginning for us and I'm excited to see where God takes this."

"As am I." Monica winked. "Now! We will go ahead and leave you alone to get ready. Talk to you soon, girl, okay? You better pick up when we answer."

"I promise I will." My girls and I shared secret smiles, as we hugged a final time, and then parted ways—Monica and Tatyana to embark on the journeys of their careers, and me to spend time with the best family on this side of Heaven. We planned to go down to The Alcove, fly back up to the Smoky Mountains to Mrs. Callie's cottage, and then come back home to restart our new life officially.

I was ecstatic and could hardly help myself as I showered quickly, and then dressed just as promptly in jeans and a sweater, and then literally skipped downstairs in my favorite house shoes. I didn't feel like I was missing out on anything, anymore, by not joining the tour because I knew the *true* blessing was being able to navigate through another day, in the company of my husband and children.

"It smells so good in here, *mmm*," I practically groaned, as my stomach simultaneously omitted a growl.

There was a nice spread of pastries, breakfast foods, and other goodies on the table. To my surprise, my parents, Monica and Tatyana, the children, and even Saige, stared back at me with identical smiles. I hadn't seen my mother or father in a while, and especially in the same room together, thanks to the stupid coronavirus. I could feel my eyes water as our eyes caught. I ran into their arms like a little girl, first kissing my mother and then my father.

"You guys are here! Oh, my goodness! What's going on? Is everything okay?" I pulled back and touched each of their faces lovingly. "Did you guys get okayed by your doctors before travelling?"

"Honey-bae, calm down. We have both been tested and approved by our physicians to travel. Stop that! *I'm* the mother," Jeffie Lee, my headstrong mother, spoke playfully. Her greying hair was pulled up into a neat bun and a feathered bang hung slightly into her piercing hazel eyes. She wore all black and looked slim and trim as always. To me, she would forever look the same and be so beautiful to me.

I examined my father, who appeared to have slimmed down since our last get-together, as his button-up shirt barely touched his stomach except when he inhaled. His black and grey hair was short in a buzz cut, a style he wore faithfully since his Air Force days. His cheekbones and strong jaw had always made him look stern and so handsome, strong, and commanding. Yet, he was a teddy bear whenever I or his granddaughters were around.

I was thankful yet confused by my family's appearance in my home, as no one had announced to me that they were coming. I was still shocked by Monica and Tatyana's visit, and I was downright taken aback as to why the "enemy" was in my home. Saige looked uncomfortable but at least she was fully dressed and silent.

My initial thought was to charge her up and ask her why she was in our home, but I was feeling too giddy about my family being there.

Instead, I turned to Keith, giving him a questioning stare. "What's…going on, baby? I wasn't expecting company, though I'm glad most of them are here."

Keith wiped his hands on a dishtowel as he rounded the island. He was casual in jeans, bare feet, and a plain white T-shirt, fresh out of a department store pack. His arms were appetizing in the slim-fitting shirt, and if company wasn't around, I would have squeezed his muscles to my heart's content.

"Monica picked up your father from the bus station for me, and Taty met your mom at the airport earlier this morning. I invited everyone here today, which was tough actually, considering everyone's different schedules, but I knew I had to make this day special for you."

"Special for me? But it's *your* birthday coming up, baby. You didn't have to—"

"I know I didn't, but I did. I wanted to. Just listen," he instructed gently, grabbing my hands in his. I searched his face, still in awe and in shock. "Baby, I had not been acting like the man you married or the man you fell in love with. Unfortunately, it took several people telling me about myself, in order for me to see how much I was hurting you. I was selfish. I put my needs first and pursued my own dreams and goals, but when it came to you, I talked you out of opportunities and made it challenging for you to do what makes you happy."

The thump of my heart was strong and monotonous in my ear. For the first time ever, I was absolutely speechless.

"Dancing makes you happy," he continued. "And whether it's my birthday, a holiday, or even a Sunday morning where we have to miss church, it's only right for me to allow you to spread your wings and do what you love regardless! This is especially true for a once in a lifetime opportunity like performing on prime time. So..."

I watched him back away and pick up a thin strip of fabric that was on the countertop. He held it in his hands, while wiggling his eyebrows playfully, as he approached me again. "Here's the deal. You have to promise me you won't worry about the kids or home duties, or anything else like that. I just want you to focus on the job you've been hired to do."

I was still confused by everything, though my heart felt full. I closed my eyes as he placed the cloth around my face, shielding my vision. I could feel him lightly tying the fabric into a knot at the back of my head, and then moving his hand in front of my face a few times. "See anything?"

"Nothing but darkness," I told him.

"Good. Come on...let's walk, baby. I want to show you something."

Wrapped in Keith's arms, he walked forward and I had no choice but to follow suit as he led me through the house and outside. I could feel the crispness of the morning air on my skin, and shivered a little.

I soon felt Keith's full lips against my temple, kissing once and then twice. Then he whispered, "Alright, 'Low. You can remove the blindfold only under one condition."

"What's that?"

"You tell me you love me, and how I'm the best husband in the world like you used to do when we first got married."

I giggled and repeated the phrase to him.

"That's my girl. Okay, take off the blindfold."

I did as told and had to blink a few times to clear the dancing speckles in front of my eyes. Once my vision was focused, I had the perfect view of the biggest, brightest colored tour bus I'd ever seen before. It was mostly white and light blue with painted images of fluffy clouds throughout the design. I *loved* clouds.

As I looked closer, I could spot the words *"The Marlow Richmond Dance Company"* in cursive, in a frosted bright blue color. A driver sat in the front seat, waving at me, and fully packed duffel bags—ones that I had intended for our family trip—were gathered in front of the entrance of the bus.

"You...you bought me a *tour bus*?"

"I did." Keith glared down at me with love in his eyes. It was an emotion I had not seen in a long while. Support. Unconditional love and unwavering support. "That way, you can ride in style and comfort as you go down to Tampa for rehearsals with your girls. Have fun, baby."

"But...but your trip...and the kids…and…"

He shook his head and placed a finger to my babbling mouth. "There will be more family vacations later on. Go out and be great, baby. Don't let me or anyone else stop you anymore. Remember? This has been your dream since you were a little girl."

I had tears in my eyes as I jumped into his unexpected arms and held onto him like a little girl would her father. I kissed his cheek and mouth over and over again, and enjoyed the delicious clean scent of his aftershave. Tears of gratitude were warm as they cascaded down my cheeks, spilling over onto our shirts collectively.

"Aw, don't make me start crying, girl. You know how I get. Hold up. There's one more thing..."

I was overwhelmed from all of the surprises. Any more would cause me to burst, I was convinced. Still, I pulled back, and listened with grateful ears as he cupped his hands around my hips and gave me further instructions.

"When you come back from dancing and recording the prime time special, your little corner studio by Shalom's favorite downtown play area will be waiting for you."

He dug around in one of his pockets and came away with a set of shiny silver keys that seemed to glisten with newness. He dangled them before me and then gently placed them inside of my trembling hand.

"Years ago, I robbed you of the opportunity to teach the youth in performing arts. This studio will hopefully make up for that selfishness. It's all yours...paid in full..."

"Keith...baby...how did you...?" I cried into my available hand, unable to formulate a complete sentence. "This is just...so awesome and unexpected and overwhelming. Oh, my goodness."

"I know you aren't necessarily a fan of hers, but you have Saige to thank for the studio. She was originally going to sell it to me for another athletic center, but the words of a good friend changed my thinking."

As he said *good friend*, his eyes locked with Tatyana's, and something told me the two had probably connected and talked recently.

Keith continued, "Instead of always thinking about me for a change, baby, it is my honor to give you the keys to your own personal sanctuary. When you come back from rehearsing and recording on prime time, and touring with your girls, your family will be there always to support you, baby. We're stuck like glue."

"So I'm stuck wit'chu for an eternity, huh?"

"Like glue, baby," he repeated, gathering me in his arms again and kissing me senselessly in front of our friends, family, and neighbor.

I thanked God right then and there for our renewed marriage and friendship, for my babies and other family and good friends, and for the thoughtfulness behind this entire trip.

I knew in my heart of hearts that we would be okay. We were going to make it. No matter what life threw our way, our family was strong enough to persevere. We had been through hopefully the worst of the storm and had good things and greatness waiting for us on the other side.

You're back in my good grace,
I'm back in your embrace.
This love story is far from done,
But your heart I'll forever chase.
It's...
Crazy how we spoke of divorce and separation,
But God said otherwise.
It's...
Ironic how we spoke of splitting up,
But fate cannot lie.
We were meant for each other,
Forever and ever we will be.
Suffice it to say, baby,
**Will you remarry me?**

**THE END**

Thank you for reading! **Please consider leaving a review on Amazon/Goodreads, and/or write to the author herself at** *info@osrbooks.com*. Reviews and word-of-mouth recommendations mean EVERYTHING to the author.

*If you are discussing this short story as a book club, please refer to the below questions.*

1. Was Keith wrong for immediately dismissing Marlow's plans to tour?

2. Was Marlow wrong for putting her (once in a lifetime) career opportunity before a previously scheduled family trip?

3. Is it wrong for a parent/spouse to occasionally travel or leave the household to pursue a career opportunity?

4. Should divorce be openly discussed with children as young as David, Harlee and Shalom?

5. Why do you believe society guilt-trips parents (especially mothers) into not having a career, goals, or dreams after the children? How can a parent properly balance the two?

# ABOUT THE AUTHOR

Olivia Shaw-Reel has written nearly 30 books before her 30th birthday. Her award-winning novels, *Soul Cry, What God Has Joined Together, and Matters of the Hart: A Tale of the Dysfunctional Hart Sisters*, have become her biggest-selling books to date.

She also hosts *The Reel Love Podcast* with her husband, Paris. Olivia lives in Milwaukee, WI.

Visit the official storefront for updates and to purchase autographed paperbacks: *osrbooks.com.*

Follow her on Instagram, Clubhouse, TikTok, Facebook and Twitter *@oliviashawreel.*

# OTHER TITLES FROM THE AUTHOR

Soul Cry, Vol. 3
What God Has Joined Together, *2-Book Series*
Baptized in Her Seduction: A Church Love Affair,
*2-Book Series*
Lord, Save Me From Myself, *2-Book Series*
Meet Me at the Altar
Full Court Mess
The Only Gift
Andrue & Sy'mone: An Urban Love Affair, *3-
Book Series*
Can't Leave Him Alone After the Love We Made,
*Book 1*
Sins of a Mafia Princess
Matters of the Hart: A Tale of the Dysfunctional
Hart Sisters, *3-Book Series*
In Love With Everything You Could Be
Stalked by My Pastor, *Book 1*
A Christmas Miracle
Who's Loving You This Christmas?
Saved, Sanctified, & Filled With Anxiety
Compilation

www.ingramcontent.com/pod-product-compliance
Lightning Source LLC
Chambersburg PA
CBHW070820250626
47170CB00006B/2171